D0892025

G.K. CHESTERTON

SEVEN SUSPECTS

SELECTED AND ARRANGED BY

Marie Smith

Foreword by H.R.F. Keating

First published in Great Britain by Xanadu Publications Limited 1990
First published in the United States of America by Carroll & Graf Publishers, Inc. 1990, by arrangement with Xanadu Publications Ltd

Carroll & Graf Publishers, Inc.
260 Fifth Avenue
New York, NY 10001

Library of Congress Cataloguing-in-Publication Data

Chesterton, G. K. (Gilbert Keith), 1874–1936
Seven Suspects / G. K. Chesterton. – 1st Carroll & Graf ed.
p. cm.
Includes bibliographical references
Contents. The man who shot the fox – The five of swords – The noticeable conduct of Professor Chadd – The moderate murder – The tower of treason – The purple jewel – The vanishing prince
ISBN 0-88184-578-7 $17.95
1. Detective and mystery stories. English. I. Title.
PR4453.c4S47 1990
823'.912 – dc20

90-31453
CIP

Manufactured in Great Britain

CONTENTS

INTRODUCTION

By H. R. F. Keating

Rarities revived: how often when one comes to read such pieces does the damning thought leap to mind 'Yeah, and I can well see why it was a rarity.' But with G.K. Chesterton the very opposite idea springs up. How extraordinary, one almost always finds oneself thinking, that in just a few sentences the man can stamp out something so alive, vibrant with a unique style. Take the very first words of the first story in this collection of revived rarities – and 'The Man Who Shot the Fox' is a rarity indeed, never reprinted since its first magazine appearance in the 1920s, unlisted in the bibliographies – words seemingly of simply, unadorned description. *The Rev. David East was walking with a companion up the single steep street that constituted almost the whole village of Windover.* Yet somehow just in those twenty-two words somcething curious, individual, different, compelling, comes to life.

For one thing, the words contrive to paint a remarkably vivid picture and vividness – almost hallucinatory vividness – is one of the sign-manuals of Chesterton's genius. Perhaps that vividness is produced here by the phrase 'single steep street' or even by that key word 'steep'. Chesterton has seen the scene with the full bite of his imagination: despite the ordinariness of the words he uses, we see it in his steps. And then there is that other simple, brief description 'with a companion'. Who is this?, one asks at once. The cunning storyteller has laid his first trap. But more. The clergyman is not walking with 'a friend' or 'another man' or simply 'another'. He is walking with 'a companion'. The word implies much. Not only do we want to know who this other person is, as we would in the hands of any good storyteller, we already get a hint of something extra, of something almost mystical. The other figure in that scene evoked with so few strokes is, we vaguely feel, a member of a companionship, of a body of people somehow set apart.

Am I reading too much into those twenty-two ordinary words? I do not think so. And as you read on I think you will find the unique Chestertonian atmosphere, more obviously present in other passages, does after all reside in that single sentence, seemingly so ordinary. As additional evidence I can perhaps cite something Hilaire Belloc once wrote about Chesterton. He was describing how he was reading to him a novel he had just completed and, he says, as soon as the outline of the tale was clear Chesterton took paper and sketched with a soft pencil 'in gestures that were like caresses sometimes, sometimes like commands, sometimes like rapier-thrusts, the whole of what a man or woman was.' It is the same uncanny gift.

Each of these stories is, you will find, similarly illuminated by the pen pictures this writer (who was also no mean artist) dashes down. They are wildly vivid, far from penny plain, not even twopence coloured but, shall we say, fourpence fantastical. And as such they take us into a unique world. But it is a world that always reflects the world we live in and have to battle our way through. Were it not so these stories would deserve to become those rarities that ought to remain lost in the pages of obscure magazines. But Chesterton always could not help writing for more than money, though he was in his charmingly bohemian way frequently short of that necessary stuff and resorted to his pen to acquire a little more. Yet once embarked on a story he was incapable of not putting the whole of himself into it. So what might seem to be the most everyday tale of quick detection gets to be a morality story in miniature, the manifesto of a man setting forth the way he thinks the world should be. And he does it not only for his time but for all time.

Note how often the paradoxical points Chesterton made long ago now seem to apply to the particular circumstances of our day. Look how in that tale of duelling and death in the grounds of a French chateau, 'The Five of Swords', there is a passage about big businesses that sends a rapier-thrust into the takeovers times we live in today. Or, reading 'The Noticeable Conduct of Professor Chadd', ponder for a moment what Chesterton makes his sleuth, Basil Grant, whose other adventures were collected as long ago as 1905 in *The Club of Queer Trades*, say about the attitude of a certain sort of Radical (We call them liberals now) towards Zulus (We say blacks now), an attitude substituting a bloodless championship for actual sympathy. Don't you know some contemporary examples? Are you, perhaps, one yourself? Or, again, there is an almost sickening piece of prophecy in 'The Tower of Treason', when Chesterton points to violence used by 'Orangemen as well as Fenians'. Only the latter have changed their name in our day in Northern Ireland to the I.R.A.

But the title of this collection is *Seven Suspects*,and it is fair to ask how the stories rate, not as fantasies with an ever-relevant moral backbone, but as what they seem on the surface to be and what Chesterton set out to produce: tales of detection. I think they rate, in fact, pretty high, as one might expect of the author of the Father Brown stories, a handful of which still shine as brilliant examples of the literary game of fooling the reader.

To begin with, all of these seven stories, and almost all of the crime stories Chesterton ever wrote, are splendid pieces of storytelling. You want to know what will happen next every bit as much as you want to know what will happen in the end. Storytelling is a gift shared by many other forms of fiction, but it is a necessity, I believe, in all detective fiction. Without it detection becomes absolutely a game, to be as easily abandoned as a game of draughts. With that tug of the good story, detection becomes something a little more, something you can't put down and something that is likely to lodge for ever in some deep nook of our memories.

But there is more to Chesterton as a detective-story writer than fine storytelling. He may not employ the tricks as frequently as, say, Agatha Christie, but he uses them every bit as adroitly. 'The Tower of Treason' looked at in this prosaic light is as good a locked-room story, or perhaps to be fair nearly as good, as that great classic of the sub-genre, Jacques Futrelle's

'The Problem of Cell 13'. The three questions Father Stephen asks in the same story are every bit as mysterious and as subtly revealing as Sherlock Holmes's famous teaser about 'the dog in the night-time'. While in the business of placing the clues – I won't point any out to spoil your pleasure – Chesterton is as neat and as cunning when he wants to be as Conan Doyle and Christie put together.

Paradox, that hallmark of the Chestertonian approach, is, as it happens, almost as important a weapon in the detective-story writer's armoury as is cunning with clues or locked-room ingenuity. The essence of the detective story, one could say, is the sudden realisation that something we thought was the right way up has been seen upside-down. And this is precisely what a paradox is. 'If a thing is worth doing,' Chesterton said most famously, 'it is worth doing badly.' And, yes, after a moment of shock, one agrees.

In these stories that sort of paradox, which seems to have come as naturally as breathing to Chesterton, abounds. Nowhere more so, perhaps, than in the story 'The Moderate Murderer' – itself a paradox – in which Chesterton consciously refers to the effect of the device. Tom, the mildly sub-normal boy in it, remarks of its unlikely 'detective' John Hume, 'He says silly things just to make you think.' How often, and how effectively, Chesterton himself does just that. Elsewhere, too, John Hume talks about 'the educational effect of riddles'; the childish-seeming, even irritating, dictum that, pondered over a little, suddenly casts a wider light. Riddles, too, are a classic device of the detective story. Homes's dog in the night-time, again.

So, put together, the cunning over the perhaps childish elements of the pure detective story, and the fundamental and often still applicable seriousness of the moral writer make for us, in these rarities as in the far better-known Father Brown tales, something that proves to be marvellously enjoyable. And what could be more desirable than that?

A DEFENCE OF DETECTIVE STORIES

By G. K. Chesterton

In attempting to reach the genuine psychological reason for the popularity of detective stories, it is necessary to rid ourselves of many mere phrases. It is not true, for example, that the populace prefer bad literature to good, and accept detective stories because they are bad literature. The mere absence of artistic subtlety does not make a book popular. Bradshaw's *Railway Guide* contains few gleams of psychological comedy, yet it is not read aloud uproariously on winter evenings. If detective stories are read with more exuberance than railway guides, it is certainly because they are more artistic. Many good books have fortunately been popular; many bad books, still more fortunately, have been unpopular. A good detective story would probably be even more popular than a bad one. The trouble in this matter is that many people do not realise that there is such a thing as a good detective story; it is to them like speaking of a good devil. To write a story about a burglary is, in their eyes a sort of spiritual manner of committing it. To persons of somewhat weak sensibility this is natural enough; it must be confessed that many detective stories are as full of sensational crime as one of Shakespeare's plays.

There is, however, between a good detective story and a bad detective story as much, or, rather more, difference than there is between a good epic and a bad one. Not only is a detective story a perfectly legitimate form of art, but it has certain definite and real advantages as an agent of the public weal.

The first essential value of the detective story lies in this, that it is the earliest and only form of popular literature in which is expressed some sense of the poetry of modern life. Men lived among mighty mountains and eternal forests for ages before they realised that they were poetical; it may reasonably be inferred that some of our descendants may see the chimney-pots as rich a purple as the mountain-peaks, and find the lamp-posts as old and natural as the trees. Of this realisation of a great city itself as something wild and obvious the detective story is certainly the *Iliad*. No one can have failed to notice that in these stories the hero or the investigator crosses London with something of the loneliness and liberty of a prince in a tale of elfland, that in the course of that incalculable journey the casual omnibus assumes the primal colours of a fairy ship. The lights of the city begin to glow like innumerable goblin eyes, since they are the guardians of some secret, however crude, which the writer knows and the reader does not. Every twist of the road is like a finger pointing to it; every fantastic skyline of chimney-pots seems wildly and derisively signalling the meaning of the mystery.

This realisation of the poetry of London is not a small thing. A city is, properly speaking, more poetic even than a countryside, for while nature is a chaos of unconscious forces, a city is a chaos of conscious ones. The crest of the flower or the pattern of the lichen may or may not be significant symbols. But there is no stone in the street and no brick in the wall that is not actually a deliberate symbol – a message from some man, as much as if it were a telegram or a post card. The narrowest street possesses, in every crook and twist of its intention, the soul of the man who built it, perhaps long in his grave. Every brick has as human a hieroglyph as if it were a graven brick of Babylon; every slate on the roof is as educational a document as if it were a slate covered with addition and subtraction sums. Anything which tends, even under the fantastic form of the minutiae of Sherlock Holmes, to assert this romance of detail in civilisation, to emphasise this unfathomably human character in flints and tiles, is a good thing. It is good that the average man should fall into the habit of looking imaginatively at ten men in the street even if it is only on the chance that the eleventh might be a notorious thief. We may dream, perhaps, that it might be possible to have another and higher romance of

London, that men's souls have stranger adventures than their bodies, and that it would be harder and more exciting to hunt their virtues than to hunt their crimes. But since our great authors (with the admirable exception of Stevenson) decline to write of that thrilling mood and moment when the eyes of the great city, like the eyes of a cat, begin to flame in the dark, we must give fair credit to the popular literature which, amid a babble of pedantry and preciosity, declines to regard the present as prosaic or the common as commonplace. Popular art in all ages has been interested in contemporary manners and costume; it dressed the groups around the Crucifixion in the garb of Florentine gentlefolk or Flemish burghers. In the last century it was the custom for distinguished actors to present Macbeth in a powdered wig and ruffles. How far we are ourselves in this age from such conviction of the poetry of our own life and manners may easily be conceived by any one who chooses to imagine a picture of Alfred the Great toasting the cakes dressed in tourist's knickerbockers, or a performance of *Hamlet* in which the prince appeared in a frock-coat, with a crape band round his hat. But this instinct of the age to look back, like Lot's wife, could not go on for ever. A rude, popular literature of the romantic possibilities of the modern city was bound to arise. It has arisen in the popular detective stories, as rough and refreshing as the ballads of Robin Hood.

There is, however, another good work that is done by detective stories. While it is the constant tendency of the Old Adam to rebel against so universal and automatic a thing as civilisation, to preach departure and rebellion, the romance of police activity keeps in some sense before the mind the fact that civilisation itself is the most sensational of departures and the most romantic of rebellions. By dealing with the unsleeping sentinels who guard the outposts of society, it tends to remind us that we live in an armed camp, making war with a chaotic world, and that the criminals, the children of chaos, are nothing but the traitors within our gates. When the detective in a police romance stands alone, and somewhat fatuously fearless amid the knives and fists of a thieves' kitchen, it does certainly serve to make us remember that it is the agent of social justice who is the original and poetic figure, while the burglars and footpads are merely placid old cosmic conservatives, happy in the immemorial respectability of apes and wolves. The romance of the police force is thus the whole romance of man. It is based on the fact that morality is the most dark and daring of conspiracies. It reminds us that the whole noiseless and unnoticeable police management by which we are ruled and protected is only a successful knight-errantry.

1

THE MAN WHO SHOT THE FOX

The Rev. David East was walking with a companion up the single steep street that constituted almost the whole village of Wonover. Even on that sunny afternoon the street was practically empty in front of him except for two figures walking far ahead; in whom indeed (as it happened) he was sufficiently interested to have picked them out even in a crowd. But if he had been in a mood for idler fancies he might have pictured, fleeing in fantastic rout before him, a whole mob of mythological animals.

For that string of houses had once been something very like a string of public-houses. Each house was now a monument of his victory over something that was for him a monster; and one that had been displayed on an escutcheon above the street, in the manner of a heraldic monster. He might well have prided himself on having played lion-tamer to the Red Lion and pig-sticker to the Blue Boar, Deer-slayer to the White Hart and St George to the Green Dragon.

When David East began his eager ministry in those parts, the hamlet was almost built of hostelries; and the citizens would seem to have lived, not by taking in each other's washing, but by giving an earnest and enthusiastic preacher of the simple life; and it would be preferable, perhaps, if we could say that his eloquence had converted all that crowd of villagers, as it might well have done in any place where Puritanism has been a real popular tradition. But this was Old England, and a very old part of it, the Downs of Wessex; and he had needed to convert only one man: the man who walked at his side.

For the man was Sir Arthur Irving, the young squire who owned all that village, not had he himself required much conversion. He had come from Cambridge with a youthful seriousness about his responsibilities as a social reformer; he was a young man of many intellectual tastes and even talents, including a talent for landscape-painting – which explained the light easel and camp-stool he was at that moment carrying to a sketching place on the hills beyond. In appearance he was tall and dark, with features distinguished and even handsome save for a slight elongation that would have been called equine in a caricature – a type that often goes with silence and generally with solemnity.

His companion, the Reverend David, was also tall and capable of a fairly continuous silence; but there the resemblance ceased. He was older than the squire, and his flaxen hair was blanched prematurely even for his age; the face under it looked boyish and even babyish, until a second glance showed something resolute in the round chin and in the short nose something of a dog like pertinacity, which unconsciously accompanied the politeness and even mildness of his manner. And in his face, as compared with the landscape painter's, there was a vividness which might between talent and genius.

Sir Arthur looked as if he had not spoken for months; but East, however silent, always looked as if he had just that instant spoken, or was just about to speak. A fanciful critic might have suggested that he never slept. And indeed a certain silent vigilance and ubiquity was his strength in all social work; he never lost a link in a labyrinthine network of religious and political engagements.

What East saw before him, in the street swept clear of its signs, was, however, one of his easiest though one of his largest triumphs. And yet at the very end of the straggling street, where the trees began to appear in a ragged fringe from over the brow of the hill, there was one sign left, and a strange one. Above the door of the last house, suspended from a short pole, hung a real fox's brush; and, as Hood and a healthy age of punsters might have put it, thereby hangs this tale.

At that moment, however, David East was not thinking of his victories over the signs that had vanished or even of any defeat symbolized in the one sign that had remained. During his short speech and his long silence, his bright eyes had remained fixed on one of the two figures walking ahead – a feminine figure, that of the squire's sister, who was walking with a young man named Swayne. All four of the pedestrians had started out together, from the gates of the great country seat in the valley behind them, meaning to proceed together to the squire's sketching ground for a sort of light picnic. But Swayne and Mary Irving had insensibly drawn ahead; while the eyes of the men behind continued to follow them.

The mild and patient persistency which marked East's manner was at present that of the lover and not the reformer; and his friend the squire would have been much more comfortable if he had been talking to the reformer. For he himself was the sort of English squire who is perhaps all the more English for being the very reverse of bluff and hearty, but who is national only in a very negative way. It was perhaps something sensitive in him that made him fully himself only when things were going smoothly. They were not going smoothly now.

'I am very much distressed about this,' he said, clearing his throat uncomfortably. 'I am very much honoured, of course, and all that. I have the greatest regard for you and your work, but I am very sorry this has happened. It can't altogether depend on me, you see; and the truth is, I fancy my sister – Well, the situation is a very delicate one to deal with.'

If he had merely been at the Cambridge Union reconstructing the British Empire or in the House of Commons altering the hearths and homes of millions of his poor fellow-creatures, he would have been a weighty, polished, and fluent speaker. But as it only affected himself, his sister, and his friend (and perhaps another friend walking ahead), he was only an English gentleman, a much pleasanter thing, and gaped and floundered like fish.

East was still gazing steadily ahead at the two figures which began to draw towards the dark fringe of the woods against an edge of evening sky.

'You mean,' he remarked quietly, 'that I am too late.'

'I have no right to say that,' replied Irving. 'But I do fancy I know enough to be rather sorry about this.'

'Mr Swayne is a lawyer, I think,' observed East with as much composure as if he had been changing the subject.

'Well, he is a barrister, I believe,' answered the young squire, 'but I don't think he does much at that or gets most out of it. He's written several novels that have sold pretty well, I fancy. Mostly about murders, I think. For the rest he's a sort of free-lance journalist, but very consistent in his opinions; in fact, I should describe him as a rabid romantic. It's absurd for people to call him an adventurer; he's a very good family, and all that. But he's – well, I'm afraid he doesn't often listen to your sermons.'

'So far as I know,' replied East, with quiet contempt, 'you are the only man of very good family who ever will listen to them.'

Sir Arthur accepted the tribute rather hastily, for he was not unconscious of the abnormality of the social position. It is very rare indeed, in such a village of South England, that the chapel has grown greater than the church; but the circumstances in this case were peculiar. The Irving family had come from the industrial North only in the last generation, and the old squire, Sir Caleb Irving, had brought his religion with him. In fact (and the fact is far from rare), the old squire was really a new squire, and only an old merchant. But at least he had a new religion; indeed, he had had several new religions.

Nor was the religion preached by the Rev. David East, which had caught the old man late in life and in a mood of sincere penitence, by any means unworthy or unsuitable to a sincere penitent. If it concerned itself, like certain other Puritanic beliefs, largely with the prophetic books and with the divine cryptogram of the Apocalypse, it interpreted them in a very practical and even political fashion, translating every opened seal as a modern emancipation, and every vial of wrath as the result of a social sin.

It was probably an exaggeration or perversion of their meaning which represented them as explaining the vision of wheels in Ezekiel as the success of modern machinery. And it can not be called less than libel to say, as so many said, that these simple believers regarded the beasts with many eyes as the best types of ideal government inspectors. Nor was there a word of truth in the absurd assertion that they explained the symbols of baptism by water and fire as meaning the necessity of hot and cold water in the bathrooms.

Sir Arthur frowned as he remembered these ridiculous, not to say rebellious, rumours. He knew from whom all such jokes originally came: from the one spot that was now his eyesore, from the one man who still remained an incongruous figure in that landscape, and who, a few hundred yards up the road in front of them, stood at his own front door under the sign of the fox's tail.

By the time they reached the brow of the hill, where the straggling houses and the woods began, the gold of evening had already reddened into copper, and sparks of it, here and there low down amid the dark woods, had the look rather of rubies. It was indeed the time and tint of sunset which Irving had carried his easel all that way to copy; but at that moment his gaze was not fixed only on the sunset.

The couple walking ahead had already paused to await his coming; and their two figures on the brow of the hill, dark against the red and orange glow, were alone suggestive of all the suspicions that had caused him to withhold hope from his companion. The attitudes were almost conventional, and quite conversational; yet it seemed impossible to doubt the nature of the conversation.

The Rev. David East seemed to take it very quietly, with head bent but eyes still bright and steady. It was not till long afterwards that Irving wholly understand the look in his face; but some part of it he understood only a few moments afterwards, with not a little amazement. For as he advanced, the group of two broke up and his sister came hurriedly towards him.

She was much smaller and slighter than her brother and much

better-looking; being beautiful in the dark fashion in which he was only handsome, but also in a tragic fashion where he was only solemn. At this moment she looked especially tragic; and there was alive in her eyes that anxiety which is generally feminine, and comes of the co-existence of duty and doubt. She was of the sort that could be a martyr to her own faith, but only a sceptic about her own martyrdom.

But it was only a glimpse of this tragic mask that was given to her brother; for, very much to his surprise, she hurriedly excused herself from the party, saying she had forgotten to call at the carpenter's cottage opposite; into which she had vanished before her brother had recovered from his bewilderment.

The next moment he found himself drawn apart by his friend Philip Swayne; and was still more surprised to find that gentleman, whose levity he had generally reason to lament, was now sobered by some similar shock. Swayne was tall, lean, and active, with red tufts of eyebrow and mustache and a shrewd, humorous blue eye. But just now his red hair looked redder against an unnatural pallor, and his face looked not only lean but haggard. He carried an ordinary sportsman's gun in his left hand at the moment, and he held out his right hand, as if in farewell.

'Good-by, old chap,' he said abruptly. 'I've hung about here too long, and now I must bring my visit to an end anyhow. If you don't mind, I'll blaze away in your woods a bit to relieve my feelings, and then get down to the station. I confess I feel rather in the mood for shooting something; not to say shooting somebody.'

'I don't understand,' remonstrated the young squire. 'Have you and Mary quarrelled? I thought that she –

'Yes, yes,' said Swayne gloomily. 'I may be a fool, but I'm afraid I thought that she – Indeed, I can't yet shake off the notion that she thought that she – But anyhow, for some reason or other, it's all up; and the less I say about it the better.'

The Rev. David East was standing some distance away, with head bent seriously after his habit, studying the pebbles on the road. But even as Swayne uttered his last, bitter words, the girl came out of the carpenter's cottage and headed hurriedly down the road towards her home; but David East had looked across at her once, and smiled.

Before Irving could turn again to speak to him, Swayne had waved his head with a farewell gesture, and, leaping clean over a bush by the roadside, had soon vanished into the first fringe of the woods.

From the little house by the edge of the woods, where the fox's tail hung above the door, there came a burst of riotous laughter and singing, of an unseemly sort which had not been heard in the model village since the signs had been swept from its street.

'It's that scoundrel serving out beer and brandy still!' exclaimed the squire, angrily. 'I can't think why my father put up with him; I swear I'll not put up with him any longer.'

'Your father did put up with him,' said East gently. 'He made special provision for him when we cleared away the other public-houses. I confess I still think that ought to restrain you.'

'I'm damned if I'll stand this any longer,' he said. 'I'll turn him out today.'

Sir Arthur might have wavered for an instant in his indignant advance on the little house if a derisive voice from its doorway had not decided him. Outside the house, and immediately under its hairy sign, stood a rough bench and table such as are often found on the frontage of old inns; and on the bench, with his elbow on the table, sat the smiling proprietor of this irregular hostelry. His appearance was as strange as a living scarecrow's, for his raven-coloured hair stood out in long crooked wisps like the ruffled or broken feathers of a raven; his lean high-featured face was bronzed like a gypsy's; and his patched and tattered clothes seemed to be hardly held together by a broad, shabby old leather belt.

But it was perhaps the most fantastic fact of all that out of this walking rubbish heap of rags and bones came the incongruous accent of an educated man.

'May I offer you a glass of ale, gentlemen?' he called out very coolly. 'Mr East, it will have a most inspiriting effect on your eloquence.'

'Look here!' burst in the young squire. 'I've come here to end all this nonsense; and what's more, I'll not have Mr East talked to in this impudent fashion in the village. He's a better man than any of you beasts are ever likely to be; and you'd much better learn a few cleaner ideas from him.'

'I am sure he is a perfect Galahad,' drawled the man leaning on the table, 'and calculated at any moment to follow the Gleam and go after the Holy Grail. But really, I am very unfortunate today! I should not have mentioned the Holy Grail, of course. How difficult you must find it to expurgate all the legend and literature of the world! And how unfortunate it is that the Christian Sacrament itself did not take the form of lemonade – !'

'If you blaspheme, it about finishes it for me,' said the squire furiously. 'Look here! I know nothing about you, except that my father called you Martin Hook, and let you hang on at this place for some reason I could never comprehend. I respect my father's memory; but I also respect myself and the people of this village; and there's a limit to everything. I'll give you the ordinary notice, though I'm bound even to do that; but you must clear out of this.'

The man called Hook put one claw-like hand on the table and took a flying leap over it. When he stood in front he was transfigured; all his lounging and sneering manner had dropped from him, and he spoke like an insulted gentleman.

'I shall not need your notice,' he said. 'Long ago I swore that if ever such a word was spoken to me, I would walk away on the spot; and if ever I walked away, I would never return. You shall never see me again, and I will never see you again; and perhaps it is as well. I will only stop to collect a few things.'

He strode into the house with his new air of energy while they stood wondering outside. A rummaging about was heard in the dark and dismal interior. He reappeared with a sort of light luggage more fantastic than his clothes: a gun under his arm, a bottle of brandy sticking out of his pocket, some ragged books stuffed into the other pocket; and balanced in one hand a big packet of parchments or papers tied with red tape and yellow seals. But this last, was the greatest surprise of all; for with a gesture like a conjurer's he sent the packet flying through the air in the direction of the squire, who had to forget his dignity and catch it like a cricket-ball.

Before he was free of the mere automatic accuracy of the act, the strange man who threw it was looking down on him from the steep bank behind the house, which was clothed with the beginning of a pine wood. Standing against the grey and purple shadows of the pine-trunks, his figure had something unearthly beyond all its ugly details; he looked at least as outlandish as a red Indian. And it was out of such a twilight, seeming indescribably distant and disconnected, that his voice came for the last time.

'Good-by, Sir Arthur,' he said. 'I am going far away from your village – possibly to starve; more probably to steal. Under these circumstances, I thought I would leave a piece of information with you. I am your brother.'

The squire continued to stare at the grey and purple shadows of the pine-wood; but there were only the shadows to be seen. The first thing that snapped the long strain of the silence was the voice of David East, and his words sounded strange.

'What a sunset!' he said suddenly. 'Real red sunsets are common enough in books; but they are very rare in sketch books – at least in genuine sketch books like yours. That sky is the sort of thing you'll never see again all your life.'

'Did you hear what that ruffian said?' articulated the squire at last. 'What the devil has the sunset got to do with it?'

'It has nothing to do with it. That is why I mentioned it,' answered East quietly. 'Believe me, when you've had a shock, the very best thing is to go on doing exactly what you were going to do before. If you're thrown out of a cab, you should immediately get into another. If you were going to paint the evening sky, you'd better go and paint the evening sky. I'll put up your easel.'

'It's no good,' said Irving. 'I can't do anything. It's not worth the trouble of getting out the sketching-block.'

'I will get out your sketching-block,' replied East.

'I don't even feel as if I could take the old sketch off it,' went on Sir Arthur. 'A rotten sketch, too.'

'I will take the old sketch off,' said the other.

'It's getting too dark to begin all over again,' murmured Irving, distractedly, 'and my pencil's broken.'

'I will sharpen your pencil,' replied David East.

He had already fished out the block from the artist's materials, along with pencils and a big Swedish knife, with which he first slit off the top sheet of cartridge paper, and then proceeded calmly to sharpen the pencil. Sir Arthur Irving had a sense of soft and steady pressure, from a will he had never consciously appreciated before. He turned mechanically to stare at the blank white paper set up for him; and then at the great semicircular theatre of the wooded hills enriched by the deepening tints of the sunset.

As he did so, there came in the utter stillness the crack and detonation of a gun. He swung round with the very sound of it; but he was already too late. The Rev. David East had fallen all his length, with his face sunken among the grass and bracken; and the fingers which were spread out, still touching the half-sharpened pencil and the knife, seemed almost to stiffen as Irving looked down at them. He had an instinctive and instantaneous knowledge that the man was dead. And amid all the immeasurable emotions that towered up in him too high for his mind to grasp, the one distinct sensation was a feeling of the huge and hideous disproportion of a man being killed while he was cutting a pencil.

His next action was equally instinctive, and perhaps more irrational. He stood rigid so long as the echoes of the volley alone mocked the silence; but as they died away, he heard another sound – an unmistakable brush or scurry in the thickets just behind him, as if someone were escaping after the catastrophe. He leapt forward with renewed life, raced across the intervening space, and plunged into the wood.

He was in time to arrest a retreating figure, who stopped at the noise of pursuit, and turned a pale face over his shoulder.

It was the white face of Philip Swayne, whiter than he had seen it that day; and he felt for the first time something Mephistophelian in the almost scarlet tufts of eyebrow and mustache.

'Oh, my God!' said Irving. 'This is too horrible! Why on earth did you do it?'

'Do what?' asked Swayne shortly.

'By God, you are innocent then!' cried Irving.

'It may surprise you, but I am,' replied Swayne, 'and I think, after all these years, the bare possibility of it might have crossed your mind.'

'But who could have done it?' cried the distracted squire. 'I do beg your pardon, Swayne; but I've no time to do it properly now. For God's sake come back with me to the place at once.'

The easel stood up, a dark and crazy skeleton out of the dim bracken; and just above it, on the ridge against the afterglow, stood another dark figure, crazier than any skeleton. It was the bird of ill omen. Their fancy had already compared the figure to a raven; now it looked like the raven of the old war ballads, hovering over the battle-field above the slain.

Though it was but a black, tattered, and fantastic outline, Irving had instantly recognized the man called Martin Hook, and plunged through the undergrowth towards him. Even as he did so, the strange man made a motion with his hand that seemed as horrid as a second crime. He lifted the light gun he carried, and shook it aloft like a sword or spear – one vibrant gesture of victory and vengeance.

The man started, however, upon finding himself observed, and even dropped his gun, throwing up his hands a moment either in exultation or wonder.

The next moment the young squire had sprung on him and bore him backwards to the earth.

There was an instant of almost startling stillness; and then the struggle was renewed on the ground, the man underneath rolling and kicking so far afield that the easel was sent staggering and was finally shattered by the squire's body, flung with a crash, as if through its whole framework. The wild man of the woods regained his feet; he had also regained his gun. As Swayne, hurrying to the rescue, rushed at him in turn, he swung up the butt-end like a club; but Irving also was on his feet again and, springing from behind, wrenched it away once more. They closed on the man, and both found themselves sprawling, their momentary captive towering above them with a leg of the broken easel quivering in his hand. It was only when Swayne had seized a strap from the artistic baggage by the body, and managed to twist it round the man's wrists, that their combined strength managed to master him.

That night after dinner, the young squire sat down with characteristic seriousness, in evening dress at an elaborate and well-ordered desk, to open and study the parchment packet that had been flung into his hand at the beginning of all these wild events. He had read the papers steadily without a word; and at the end his face was of an unaltered gravity, but of an altered pallor.

Up and down the veranda outside, his sister and Philip Swayne were walking; their figures crossed the window from time to time in the moonlight. He saw the long perspectives of paths and hedges and the tall poplars on the horizon.

After staring sadly for a few moments at the moonlit garden, he struck the bell at his side. Then he scribbled a few lines on paper and sealed it up in an envelope, exactly filling the interval of time before a grey-haired servant appeared.

'Please have this delivered,' he said, 'to Sir Martin Irving. He is in the local prison.'

The manservant's heavy face almost awoke with wonder, and the hand held out for the letter hesitated. The young squire repeated firmly: 'To Sir Martin Irving, in the prison. He is the man who used to be called Martin Hook. Find out if the police will allow him to receive that letter. They will read it themselves, of course.'

And he got up and went out on to the veranda, leaving the servant with the letter in his hand.

The squire stood waiting outside the window, while Swayne and Mary Irving walked towards him. He had been apparently mistaken about their attitude before; but he felt fairly certain that he was not mistaken now. His sister's face, one never prone to exaggerate or even to express happiness, told him that some happiness at least had already come out of the tragedy in the woods. What was the nature of the obstacle that had separated the two only that morning he could not imagine, but it was clear that it had been an obstacle to the wishes of both; and that the obstacle was now removed, if only by the mad act of a murderer. And it weighed on him most heavily of all that he had now to throw another burden of trial and change and peril into the fine pose and balance of his sister's sensitive conscience.

'Mary,' he said abruptly, 'there is something I must tell you at once. Another rather terrible thing has happened.'

Philip Swayne turned easily on his heel, and tactfully strolled out of the veranda on to the lawns beyond. Mary stood still, as if looking after him, but she neither moved nor spoke.

'It is terrible to see you staring at our old park,' he said at last, rather huskily. 'For I, at any rate, may be looking at it for the last time. The long and short of it is that this place is not ours.'

After a pause he went on: 'I have just looked through all the legal papers and I fear they do establish the fact that my father had a legitimate elder son, disowned when he was about sixteen, when I was barely six and you were not born. They seem to have quarrelled because the boy shot a fox; at which my father was naturally indignant, as a country gentleman concerned for the best opinion of the county; though perhaps his indignation carried him too far. The man who shot the fox, it would seem, tells a story of his own to excuse himself. He professes that the fox was threatening those pigeons that Father used to keep.

'I can hardly believe that, for surely he need only have said so, to have it regarded as an extenuation at least; for Father was very fond of the pigeons. He does not even pretend that he mentioned the pigeons at the time, and I think they must have been an afterthought. But though I can hardly believe his excuses, I fear there is no doubt about his claims. And all that would matter very little to me, estate and all, if it weren't for this last ghastly calamity – that the man who is to bear my title is standing almost under the gallows for the murder of poor East.'

Still the girl did not move or speak, but stood with her face turned away like a statue in the moonlight. Irving began to feel her unshaken rigidity as something creepy and a new strain on his nerves.

'Mary,' he said,'are you ill? Was it too much of a shock to you?'

'No,' she replied. 'It was not a shock to me.'

'Then I don't understand what's the matter with you.'

'It was not a shock,' said the girl, 'because I knew it before. Mr East told me.'

'What? Did East know? Had that anything to do with his death? Come you must really tell me the truth,' cried Irving, exasperated with her mute and motionless attitude. 'Remember, I must still stand for the honour of the family, even if I am not the head of it. And everything that can be done by sorrow and justice is due to the man who died almost in my service.'

'Yes,' she said, after a moment's thought, 'sorrow and justice are certainly due to all the dead – even to him.'

'What do you mean?' demanded her brother.

'I say they are due even to him,' she said steadily, 'though he was a horrible man.'

'What are you saying? I thought – I thought you promised to marry him only this morning.'

'I promised to marry him because he was a horrible man,' said Mary Irving.

There was an insupportable silence; and then she said, still looking at the moonlight on the lawns:

'I think I am the kind of woman who is always doing wrong through worrying about doing right. Anyhow, I knew about it, and he knew about it, and by this time Philip knows about it, because I have told him. You are the only one of us who did not know. And as I knew that when you learned it you would give up the estate instantly –'

'Thank you,' said Irving sternly, and lifted his head.

'I thought it would kill you,' went on his sister. 'I thought all your life and hopes were bound up with this place, and that anything must be done to keep the secret. Yes, even if I had to marry a blackmailer.'

'Do you mean to tell me,' cried Irving, 'that this man I have known all my life, this man who was my father's friend, put you on the rack to torture you for such a purpose?'

'Yes,' answered the girl, and lifted her own pale face. 'He put me on the rack. But I did not speak.'

'Will you forgive me if I leave you?' said Irving, after another silence. 'I must think it out by myself, my dear, or you will have two mad brothers.'

He wandered away into the garden, pacing the paths and lawns wildly with his face white in the moon; and when Swayne found him in the plantation he might almost have passed indeed for a wild man of the woods himself. But Swayne was a healthy and humorous adviser, and it was not long before they were both back in the study again, turning over the papers in a more equable fashion and elucidating them with notes of some of Swayne's own investigations.

'His case is subtle. I think,' said Swayne. 'But have you considered his character in the light of that old affair of the fox and the pigeon? He was really quite right to kill the fox, which was in the act of eating a pigeon, and your father would have thanked him for it. But he never told your father. He preferred to drag out a squalid existence in that tumble-down tavern, alone with the one black joke of being in the right.'

'Do you mean to say,' asked Irving abruptly, 'that he could have defended himself about the –' He stopped.

'There are two little problems,' began Swayne, abruptly but calmly, 'which puzzled me about that murder. The first was the struggle we had, when he stood with his hands up and you sprang at him. You bowled him over like a ninepin. And yet, a moment afterwards, he had the strength of ten devils. We are both strong men, and it took us all our time to hold him. What do you guess from that? I will tell you my guess. I guess that he had no idea at first that you were going to attack him, and that he was not lifting his hands to attack you. It may seem mad, but it is my serious belief that he was going to embrace you.'

'Madness is hardly the word for it,' replied Irving, staring. 'Tell me what you're really driving at.'

'The other problem,' resumed Swayne calmly, 'I came upon when I picked up that strap from beside the body. I saw it only in a flash; but you'll remember that the dead man's fingers still lay lightly on the pencil and the long Swedish knife with which he had been cutting. But the knife was the wrong way round.'

'The wrong way round,' repeated Irving. Something cold began to creep through his blood.

'East was not holding it as a man holds a tool, with the point upwards. He was holding it as a man holds a dagger, with the point downwards. I do not wonder that you look at me like that. But it is best to say it, and get it over. East was shot dead at the very moment when he was about to stab you where you stood.'

Arthur Irving tried to speak; but no words came.

'You were standing with your back to him, you will remember, and giving him the very moment of opportunity. He wanted that opportunity badly, and had probably brought you over the brow of the hill out of sight of the village on purpose. He wanted it, then and there, for a very simple reason. It was his whole policy to keep your family in possession and marry into it; he knew your brother would never normally speak; and he had never calculated on his throwing you the packet of papers. If you went home and read them, his whole scheme was in ruins. If you merely died, your sister had the property and he had your sister's word.

'East was a gentleman of remarkable lucidity and presence of mind; and it was apparent to his intellect that you had better merely die. Only in the nick of time, your brother saw the gesture from the woods above. He also is a gentleman of great presence of mind; and the bullet went quicker than the knife. Your brother rushed down, in a real revulsion of feeling in favour of his own blood which he had rescued, and thinking only of a reconciliation. And he found himself again knocked down for having killed the fox when he had saved the pigeon. Only this time, by a new artistic touch, he was knocked down by the pigeon.'

A knock came at the door, and the grey-haired servant again appeared, carrying a letter on a tray. Irving opened it and read slowly the lines of bold, irregular writing that completed the story:

My Dear Brother:

You are certainly behaving handsomely; and I feel I ought to do the same. I do not in the least want your great big ugly house; and I shall be quite content to go back to my beer at the sign of the fox's brush. I feel I must be equally forgiving about the affair of the other fox I shot, though I was very much annoyed about it. I had originally intended to say nothing, and only allow you to learn the truth when you had hanged me neatly at the end of a rope. The idea affected me as humorous.

Your legal friend wanted to establish my innocence in various ways highly wounding my vanity. He offered to prove that I was not a murderer by proving, first, that I was a bad shot, which is a lie; second, that I was a lunatic, which is also a lie; and third, that I did not with cold premeditation intend to destroy the Rev. David East; which is the greatest lie and slander of all, and a gross reflection on my public spirit and sense of social reform. By elaborate lies like that he might have got me off; and by other elaborate likes like that he might equally well have got East off – probably by pleading that certain exercises with a Swedish knife were a part of Swedish drill.

But even if they hanged East, they would only have done it after artificial, interminable ceremonies intended to show he was guilty; whereas I killed him swiftly because I *knew* he was guilty. And this is what reminds me so much of our poor father and the fox. If I had put on an absurd pink coat and wasted hours in wandering about with a litter of dogs, if I had kept a lot of silly rules, almost as silly as those of a law-court, he would have thought it quite natural that I should exist only to kill foxes. But because I sacrificed a wild beast devouring our own livestock, he could see nothing except that I had broken a rule.

Under these circumstances you will excuse me if I maintain that I am not mad, but you are; that it is you and all your law-courts and hunting fields and solemn sport and fantastic "fair play" that are mad. I kill vermin when the vermin is trying to kill; and it may surprise you to learn that I regard myself as a person of considerable common sense. Anyhow, all's well that ends well, as the fox said when his tail was put back at the right end.

Yours always,
Martin Irving

Irving looked at the last sentence with a faint smile; and his eyes again wandered to the window. By this time he was alone once more; for Swayne had taken the opportunity to slip out at the open windows, and was once more walking with Mary Irving on the veranda under the moon.

2

THE FIVE OF SWORDS

It was doubtless a strange coincidence that the two friends, the Frenchman and the Englishman, should have argued about that particular subject on that particular morning. The coincidence may perhaps appear less incredible to a philosophic mind, if I add that they had argued about that subject every morning through the whole month of the walking tour that they took in the country south of Fontainebleau. Indeed, it was this repetition and variety of aspect that gave the more logical and patient mind of the Frenchman the occasion of his final criticism.

'My friend,' he said, 'you have told me many times that you can make no sense of the French duel. Permit me the observation that I can make no sense of the English criticism of the French duel. When we discussed it yesterday, for instance, you twitted me with the affair of old Le Mouton with that Jew journalist who calls himself Vallon. Because the poor old Senator got off with a scratch on the wrist, you call it a farce.'

'And you can't deny it was a farce,' replied the other stolidly.

'But now,' proceeded his friend, 'because we happen to pass the Château d'Orage, you dig up the corpse of the old count who was killed there, God knows when, by a vagabond Austrian soldier of fortune, and tell me with a burst of British righteousness that it was a hideous tragedy.'

'Well, and you can't deny it was a tragedy,' repeated the Englishman. 'They say the poor young countess couldn't live there in the shadow of it, and has sold the château and gone to Paris.'

'Paris has its religious consolations,' said the Frenchman, smiling somewhat austerely. 'But I think that it is too dangerous and too safe. If the duel is bloodless you call our poor French swordsman a fool. If it end in bloodshed, what do you call him?'

'I call him a bloody fool,' replied the Englishman.

The two national figures might have served to show how real is nationality, and how independent it is of race; or at least of the physical types commonly associated with race. For Paul Forain was tall, thin and fair, but French to the finger-tips, to the point of his imperial or the points of his long, narrow shoes, and in nothing more French than in a certain seriousness of curiosity that lifted his brow in a permanent furrow; you could see him thinking. And Harry Monk was short, sturdy and dark, and yet exuberantly English – English in his grey tweeds and in his short brown moustache; and in nothing so English as in a complete absence of curiosity, so far as was consistent with courtesy. He carried the humour, and especially the good humour, of the English social compromise with him like a costume; just as one might fancy his grey tweeds carried the grey English weather with him everywhere through those sunny lands. They were both young, and both professors at a famous French college – the one of jurisprudence, the other of English; but the former, Forain, had specialized so much in certain aspects of criminal law that he was often consulted on particular criminal problems. It was certain views of his about murder and manslaughter that had led to the recurrent disagreement about the duel. They commonly took their holidays together, and had just breakfasted at the inn of the Seven Stars half a mile along the road behind them.

Dawn had broken over the opposite side of the valley and shone full on the side of which their road ran. The ground fell towards the river in a series of tablelands like a terraced garden, and on the one just above them were the neglected grounds and sombre facade of the old château, flanked to left and right by an equally sombre facade of firs and pines, deployed interminably like the lost lances of an army long fallen into dust. The first shafts of the sun, still tinged with red, gleamed on a row of glass frames for cucumbers or some such vegetables, suggesting that the place was at least lately inhabited, and warmed the dark diamonded casements of the house itself, here and there turning a diamond into a ruby.But the garden was overgrown with clumps of wood almost as accidental as giant mosses, and somewhere in its melancholy maze, they knew, the sinister Colonel Tarnow, an Austrian soldier, since not unsuspected of being an Austrian spy, had thrust his blade into the throat of Maurice d'Orage, the last lord of that place. The park descended, and the view over the hedge was soon shut out by a great garden wall so loaded with ivies and ancient vines and creepers that it looked itself more like a hedge than a wall.

'I know you've been out yourself, and I know you're far from being a brute yourself,' conceded Monk, continuing the conversation. 'For my own part, however much I hated a man, I don't fancy I should ever want to kill him.'

'I don't know that did want to kill him,' answered the other. 'It would be truer to say I wanted him to kill me. You see, I wanted him to be *able* to kill me. That is what is not understand. To show how much I would stake on my side of the quarrel – hallo! What on earth is this?'

On the ivied wall above had appeared a figure, almost black against the morning sky, so that they could see nothing of its face, but only its one frenzied gesture. The next moment it had leapt from the wall and stood in their path, with hands spread out as if for succour.

'Are you doctors, either of you?' cried the unknown. 'Anyhow, you must come and help – a man's been killed.'

They could see now that the figure was that of a slim young man whose dark hair and dark clothes showed the abrupt disorder only seen in what is commonly orderly. One curl of his burnished black hair had been plucked across his eye by an intercepting branch, and he wore pale yellow gloves, one of which was burst across the knuckles.

'A man killed?' repeated Monk. 'How was he killed?'

The yellow-gloved hand made a despairing movement.

'Oh, the wretched old tale!' he cried. 'Too much wine, too many words, and the end next morning. But God knows we never meant it to go so far as this!'

With one of the lightning movements that lay hidden behind

his rather dry dignity, Forain had already scaled the low wall and was standing on it, and his English friend followed with equal activity and more unconcern. As soon as they stood there they saw on the lawn below the sight that explained everything, and made so wild and yet apt a commentary on their own controversy.

The group on the lawn included three other men in black frock-coats and top hats, excluded the messenger of misfortune, whose own silk hat lay rolled at random by the wall over which he had leapt. He seemed to have leapt it, by the way, with an impetuosity that spoke of a swift reaction of horror or repentance, for Forain noticed, only a yard or two along the garden wall, a garden door, which, though doubtless disused, rustily barred and blotched with lichen, would have been the natural exit of a more normal moment. But the eye was very reasonably riveted on the two figures, clad only in white shirts and trousers, round whom the rest revolved, and who must have crossed swords a moment before. One of these stood with the rapier still poised in his hand, a mere streak of white, which a keen eye might have seen to end in a spot of red. The other white-shirted figure lay like a white rag on the green turf, and a sword of the same pattern, a somewhat antiquated one, lay gleaming in the grass where it had fallen from his hand. One of his black-coated seconds was bending over him, and as the strangers approached lifted a livid face, a face with spectacles and a black triangular beard.

'It's too late,' he said. 'He's gone.'

The man stood holding the sword cast it down with a wordless sound more shocking than a curse. He was a tall, elegant man, with an air of fashion even in his duelling undress; his face, with a rather fine aquiline profile, looked whiter against red hair and a red pointed beard. The man beside him put a hand upon his shoulder and seemed to push him a little, perhaps urging him to fly. This witness, in the French phrase, was a tall, portly man with a long black beard cut as if in the square pattern of his long black frock-coat, somewhat incongruously, a monocle screwed into one eye. The last of the group, the second of the slayer's formal backers, stood motionless and somewhat apart from the rest – a big man, much younger than his comrades, and with a classical face like a statue's and almost as impassive as a statue's. By a movement common to the whole tragic company, he had removed his top hat at the final announcement, as if at a funeral, and the effect gave to English eyes a slight shock; for the young man's hair was cropped so close and so colourless that he might almost have been bald. The fashion was common enough in France, yet it seemed incongruous to the man's youth and good looks. It was as if Apollo were shaved as an Eastern hermit.

'Gentlemen,' said Forain at last, 'since you have brought me into this terrible business, I must be plain. I am no position to be pharisaic. I have all but killed a man myself, and I know that the riposte can be almost past control. I am not,' he added, with a faint touch of acidity, 'a humanitarian, who would have three men butchered with the axe of the guillotine because one has fallen by the sword. I am not an official, but I have some official influence; and I have, if I may say so, a reputation to lose. You must at least convince me that this affair was clean and inevitable like my own, otherwise I must go back to my friend and innkeeper of the Seven Stars, who will put me in communication with another friend of mine, the chief of police.'

And without further apology, he walked across the lawn and looked down at the fallen figure, a figure peculiarly pathetic because plainly younger than any of the survivors, even his second who had run for help. There was no hair on the pale face; the hair on the head was very fair and brushed in a way which Monk, with a new shock of sympathy, recognized as English. There was no doubt of the death; a brief examination showed that the sword had been sent straight through the heart.

The big man with the black beard broke the silence in reply:

'I will thank you, sir, for your candour, since I am, in some melancholy sense, your host on this occasion. I am Baron Bruno, owner of this house and grounds, and it was here at my table that the mortal insult was given. I owe it to my unfortunate friend Le Caron' – and he made a gesture of introduction towards the red-bearded swordsman, 'to say it was a mortal insult, and followed by a direct challenge. It was a charge of cheating at cards, and it was clinched by one of cowardice. I mean no harshness to the dead, but something is due to the living.'

Monk turned to the dead man's second. 'Do you support this?' he demanded.

'I suppose it's all right,' said the young man with the yellow gloves. 'There were faults on both sides.'

Then he added abruptly: 'My name is Waldo Lorraine, and I'm ashamed to say I am the fool who brought my poor friend here to play. He was an Englishman, Hubert Crane, whom I met in Paris, and meant, heaven knows, only to give a good time! And the only service I've done him is to be his second in this bloody ending. Dr Vandam here, being also a stranger in the house, kindly acted as my colleague. The duel was regular enough, I must fairly say, but the quarrel was – ' He paused, a shadow of shame darkened his dark face. 'I have to confess I was no judge of it, and have no memory but a sort of nightmare. In plain words, I had drunk too much to know or care.'

Dr Vandam, the pale man in the spectacles, shook his head mournfully, still staring at the corpse.

'I can't help you,' he said. 'I was at the Seven Stars, and only came in time to arrange for the fight.'

'My own fellow-witness, M. Valence,' observed the baron, indicating the man with the cropped hair, 'will ratify my version of the dispute.'

'Had he any papers?' asked Forain after a pause.'May I examine the body?'

There was no opposition, and, after searching the dead man and his waistcoat and coat that lay on the lawn, the investigator at last found a single letter, short but confirmatory, so far as it went, of the story told him. It was signed 'Abraham Crane,' and was plainly from the dead man's father in Huddersfield; indeed, Monk was able to recognize the name as that of a noted manufacturing magnate in the north. It merely concerned business on which the young man had been sent to Paris, apparently to confirm some contract with the Paris branch of the firm of Miller, Moss & Hartman; but the rather sharp adjuration to avoid the vanities of the French capital suggested that perhaps the father had some hint of the dissipations that had brought the son to his death. One thing only in this very commonplace letter puzzled the inquirer not a little. It ended by saying that the writer might himself be coming to France to hear the upshot of the Miller, Moss & Hartman affair, and that if so he would put up at the Seven Stars and call for his son at the Château d'Orage. It seemed odd that the son should have given the address of the very place where he was living the riotous life his father so strongly condemned. The only other object in the pockets besides the common necessaries was an old locket enclosing the faded portrait of a dark lady.

Forain stood frowning a moment, the paper twisted in his fingers; then he said abruptly: 'May I go up to your house, Monsieur le Baron?'

The baron bowed silently; they left the dead man's seconds to mount guard over his body, and the rest mounted slowly up the slope. They went the slower for two reasons – first, because the steep and straggling path was made more irregular by straggling roots of pine like the tails of dying dragons, and slippery with green slime that might have been their own green and unnatural gore; and second, because Forain stopped every now and then to take what seemed needless note of certain details of the general decay. Either the baron had not long been in possession of the place, or he cared very little for appearances.

What had once been a garden was eaten by giant weeds, and when they passed the cucumber frames on the slope Forain saw they were empty and the glass of one of them had a careless crack, like a star in the ice. Forain stood staring at the hole for nearly a minute. Entering the house by the long french windows, they came first on a round outer room with a round card-table. It might by the shape have been a turret-room, but seemed somehow as light and sunny as a summer-house, being white and gold in the ornate eighteenth-century style. But it was as faded as it was florid, and the white had grown yellow and the gold brown. At the moment this decay was but the background of the silent yet speaking drama of a more recent disorder. Cards were scattered across the floor and table, as if flung or struck flying from a hand that held them; champagne bottles stood or lay at random everywhere, half of them broken, nearly all of them empty; a chair was overturned. It was easy to believe all that Lorraine had said of the orgy that now seemed to him a nightmare.

'Not an edifying scene,' said the baron, with a sigh, 'and yet I suppose it has a moral.'

'It may appear singular,' replied Forain, 'but in my own moral problem it is even reassuring. Given the death, I am even glad of the drink.'

As he spoke he stooped swiftly and picked up a handful of cards from the carpet.

'The five of spades,' he said to Monk musingly in English, 'the five of swords, as the old Spaniards would say, I suppose. You know "spade" is "espada," a sword? the four of swords – spades, I mean. The three of spades. The – have you got a telephone here?'

'Yes – in another room, round by the other door of the house,' answered the baron, rather taken aback.

'I'll use it, if I may,' said Forain, and stepped swiftly out of the card-room. He strode across a larger and darker *salon* within, which for some reason had remained in a sterner and more antiquated style of decoration. There were antlers above him; a glimmer of armour showed on the gloom of oak and tapestry, and he saw one thing that arrested his eye as he strode towards the farther door. A trophy of two swords crossed was on one side of the fireplace, and on the corresponding place opposite the empty hooks of another. He understood why the two rapiers had seemed to be antiquated. Under the ominous empty hooks stood an ebony cabinet carved with cherubs as grotesque as goblins.

Forain felt as if the black cherubim were peering at him with a curiosity quite unangelic. He gazed a moment at the drawers of the cabinet, and passed on.

He shut the door behind him, and they heard another door close in a more distant part of the building, away towards the road that ran on the remoter side of the house. There was a silence; they could hear neither the bell nor the talk at the telephone.

Baron Bruno had dropped the glass from his eye, and was plucking a little nervously at his long dark beard.

'I suppose, sir,' he said, addressing Monk, 'we can count on your friend's feeling of honour?'

'I am certain of his honour,' said the Englishman, with the faintest accent on the possessiveness pronoun.

The surviving duellist, Le Caron, spoke for the first time, and roughly.

'Let the man telephone,' he said. 'No French jury would call this miserable thing murder. It was almost an accident.'

'One to be avoided, I think,' said Monk coldly.

Forain had reappeared, and his brow was cleared of its wrinkle of reflection. 'Baron,' he said, 'I have resolved my little problem. I will treat this tragedy as a private misfortune on one condition – that you all meet me and give me an account that satisfies me within this week, and in Paris. Say outside the Café Roncesvaux on Thursday night. Does that suit you? Is that understood? Very well, let us return to the garden.'

When they went out again through the french windows the sun was already high in heaven, and every detail of the slope and lawn below glittered with a new clarity. As they turned the corner of a clump of trees and came out above the duelling-ground, Forain stopped dead and put on the Baron's arm a hand that caught like a hook.

'My God!' he said. 'This will never do. You must get away at once.'

'What?' cried the other.

'It's been quick work,' said the investigator. 'The father's here already.'

They followed his glance down to the garden by the wall, and the first thing they saw was that the rusty old garden door was standing open, letting in the white light of the road. Then they realized that a few yards within it was a tall, lean, grey-bearded man, clad completely in black and looking like some Puritanic minister. He was standing on the turf and looking down at the dead. A girl in grey, with a black hat, was kneeling by the body, and the two seconds, as by an instinct of decency, had withdrawn to some distance and stood gazing gloomily at the ground. In the clear sunlight the whole group looked like a lighted scene on a green stage.

'Go back at once – all three of you,' said Forain almost fiercely. 'Get away by the other door. You must not meet *him*, at least.'

The Baron, after an instant's hesitation, seemed to assent, and Le Caron had already turned away. The slayer and his two seconds moved towards the house and vanished into it once more, the tall young man with the shaven head going last with a leisure that made even his long legs cynical. He was the only one of them who scarcely seemed affected at all.

'Mr Crane, I think,' said Forain to the bereaved father. 'I fear you know all that we can tell you.'

The grey-bearded man nodded; there was a certain frost-bitten fierceness about his face and something wild in the eye contrasting with the control in the features, something that seemed natural enough at such a time, but which they found afterwards to be more normal to him even in ordinary times.

'Sir,' he said, 'I have seen the end of cards and wine and the Lord's judgments for everything I feared.' Then he added, with an incongruous simplicity somehow rather tragic than comic: 'And fencing, sir. I was always against all that French fad of getting prizes for fencing. Football is bad enough, with betting and every sort of brutality, but it doesn't lead to this. You are English, I think?' he said abruptly to Monk. 'Have you anything to say of this abominable murder?'

'I say it is an abominable murder,' said Monk firmly. 'I was saying so to my friend hardly half an hour ago.'

'Ah, and you?' cried the old man, looking suspiciously at Forain. 'Were you defending duels, perhaps?'

'Sir,' replied Forain gently, 'it is no time for defending anything. If your son had fallen from a horse, I would not defend horses; you should say your worst of them. If he had been drowned in a boat, I would join you in wishing every boat at the bottom of the sea.'

The girl was looking at Forain with an innocent intensity of gaze which was curious and painful, but the father turned impatiently away, saying to Monk: 'As you are English at least, I should like to consult you.' And he drew the Englishman aside.

But the daughter still looked across at Forain without speech or motion, and he looked back at her with a rather indescribable interest. She was fair, like her brother, with yellow hair and a white face, but her features were irregular with that fairy luck that falls right once in fifty times, and then is more beautiful than beauty. Her eyes seemed as colourless as water, and yet as bright as diamonds, and when he met them the Frenchman realized, with a mounting and unmanageable emotion, that he was facing something far more positive than the laxity of the son or the limitations of the father.

'May I ask you, sir,' she said steadily, 'who were those three men with you just now? Were they the men who murdered him?'

'Mademoiselle,' he said, feeling somehow that all disguises had dropped, 'You use a harsh word, and heaven knows it is natural. But I must not stand before you on false pretences. I myself have held such a weapon and nearly done such a murder.'

'I don't think you look like a murderer,' she said calmly. 'But they did. That man with the red beard, he was like wolf – a well-dressed wolf, which is the worst part of it. And that big, pompous man – what could he be but horrible, with his big black beard and a glass in one eye?'

'Surely,' said Forain respectfully, 'it is not wicked to be well dressed, and a man might be more sinned against than sinning and still have a beard and an eyeglass.'

'Not all that big beard and that one little eyeglass,' she replied positively. 'Oh, I only saw them in the distance, but I know quite well I'm right.'

'I know you must think any duellist is a criminal and ought to be punished,' said Forain rather huskily. 'Only, having been one myself – '

'I don't,' she said. 'I think those duellists ought to be punished. And, just to prove what I mean and don't mean' – and her pale face was changed with a puzzling and yet dazzling smile – 'I want you to punish them.'

There was a strange silence, and she added quietly:

'You have seen something yourself. You have some guess, I am sure, about how they came to fight, and what was really behind it all. You know there is really something wrong, much more wrong than the quarrel about cards.'

He bowed to her, and seemed to yield like a man rebuked by an old friend.

'Mademoiselle,' he said, 'I am honoured by your confidence. And your commission.'

He straightened himself equally abruptly, and turned to face the father, who had drawn near in conversation with Monk.

'Mr Crane,' he said gravely, 'I must ask you for the moment to trust me. This gentleman, as well as other countrymen of yours to whom I can refer you, will, I think, tell you that I can be trusted. I have already communicated with the authorities, and you may even regard me in a sense as their representative. I can answer for the fact that those responsible in this dreadful affair are under observation, and that justice can effect whatever may be found to be just. If you will honour me with an appointment in Paris after Tuesday next, I can tell you more of many things that you ought to know. Meanwhile, I will make any arrangements you desire touching – formalities of respect for the dead.'

The eye of old Crane was still choleric, but he bowed, and Forain and Monk, returning the salutation, retraced their way up the path to the château. As they did so the Frenchman paused again by the cucumber frame and pointed to the broken glass.

'That's the biggest hole in the story so far,' he said; 'it gapes at me like the mouth of hell.'

'That!' exclaimed his friend. 'That might have happened any time.'

'It happened this morning,' said Forain, 'or else – anyhow, the broken bits are fresh; nothing has grown round them. And there is the mark of a heel on the soil inside. One of these men stepped straight on to the glass going down to the duelling ground. Why?'

'Oh, well,' observed Monk, 'that fellow Lorraine said he was blind drunk last night.'

'But not this morning,' replied Forain. 'And though a man blind drunk, even in broad daylight, might conceivably put his foot into a big glass frame right in front of him, I doubt if he could take it out again so neatly. If he were as drunk as that, I think the mantrap would trip and throw him, and there would be more broken glass. This does not look to me like a man who was blind drunk. It is more like a man who was blind – '

'Blind!' repeated Monk, with a quite irrational creeping of the flesh. 'But none of these men are blind. Is there any other explanation?'

'Yes,' replied Forain. 'They did it in the dark. And that is the darkest part of the business.'

Anyone who had tracked the course of the two friends on the ensuing Thursday evening, when dusk had already kindled around them the many-coloured lights of Paris, might have imagined that they had no purpose but the visiting of a variety of cafés. Yet their course, though crooked and erratic, was designed according to the consistent strategy of the amateur detective. Forain went first to see the countess, the still surviving widow of the nobleman who fell fifteen years before in a duel on the same spot. He went in a literal sense to see her, and not to call on her. For he contented himself with sitting outside the café opposite her house and playing with an *apéritif* until she came out to her carriage – a dark-browed lady, with a beauty rather fixed like a picture than still living like a flower: a portrait from a mummy-case. Then he merely glanced at the portrait in the old locket he had taken from the dead man's pocket, nodded almost approvingly, and made his way to a less aristocratic and more purely commercial part of the town. Passing rapidly along the solid street of banks and public buildings, he reached a large hotel built on the same ponderous pattern, but having the usual litter of little tables on the pavement outside. They were intercepted with ornamental shrubs and covered with an awning striped with white and purple, and at a table at the extreme corner, against the last green afterglow of evening, he saw the black bulk of Baron Bruno sitting between his two friends. The awning that shaded them just cut off the upper part of his tall black hat, and Monk had the fancy that he resembled some black Babylonian caryatid supporting the whole building; perhaps there was something Assyrian about his large square beard. The Englishman felt a subconscious temptation to share his country-woman's prejudice, but it was evident that Forain did not share it. For he sat down with the three men, and began to exhibit a very unexpected camaraderie and even conviviality. He ordered wine and pressed it upon them, passing afterwards into animated conversation, and it was not until about half an hour afterwards that our imaginary spectator, hovering on his tail, would have seen him start up with a slight return to stiffness, salute the company and resume his singular journey.

His zigzag course through the lighted city carried him first to a public telephone and then to a public office, which Monk was able to identify as the place where the dead body was awaiting medical examination. From this place he came out looking very grim, like one who has faced an ugly fact, but he said nothing and pursued his course to the police headquarters, where he was closeted for some time with the authorities. Then he crossed the river once more, walking swiftly and still in silence, and in a quiet corner of Paris struck the worn white gateway of a building that had once been an hotel in the ancient and aristocratic sense, and was now an hotel in a more commercial but particularly quiet fashion. Passing through the porch and passages, he came out on a garden so secluded that the very sunset sky seemed a private awning of gold and green like the awning of purple and silver under which the sombre baron had sat. A few guests in evening dress were scattered at tables under the trees, but Forain went swiftly past them to one table near a flight of garden steps, at which he could see a girl in grey with golden hair. It was Margaret Crane; she looked up as he approached, but she only said, as if breathlessly: 'Do you know any more about the murder?'

Before he could reply her father had appeared at the top of the steps, and Forain felt vaguely that while the girl's grey dress seemed to harmonize with everything, the rigid and rusty black of the old man's clothes remained like the protest of a Puritan in a garden of Cavaliers.

'The murder,' he repeated in a loud and harsh voice, heard everywhere: 'That's what we want to know about. This murder, sir!'

'Mr Crane,' said Forain, 'I hope you know how I feel your position, but it is only fair to warn you that in these criminal matters one must speak carefully. If it comes to a trial, your case will be none the better if you have abused these men at random, even in private. And I am bound to say, not only that the duel as a duel seems to have been regular, but that the duellists seem to be men of marked regularity.'

'What do you mean?' demanded the old man.

'I will be frank with you and own I have seen them since,' said Forain. 'Nay, I have passed a sort of festive evening with them – or what I meant to be a festive evening. But I am forced to say that they are as little festive as your own conscience could desire. Indeed, they seem to have business habits very much like your own. Frankly, I tried to make them drink and to draw them into a game of cards but the baron and his friends coldly declined, said they had appointments, and we parted after black coffee and a brief and rather curious conversation.'

'I hate them the more for that,' said the girl.

'You are quick, Mademoiselle,' observed Forain, with a growing admiration. 'I also took the matter in that spirit if only for experiment. I said bluntly to our baronial friend: "So long as I thought you were a drinking and a dicing company, I took this for a drunken accident. But let me tell you it does not look well when elderly men, themselves sober, themselves indifferent to play, get a mere boy among them and play cards with him. You know what is thought of that; it is thought that the old man takes a hand – well, rather too like an old hand. And it is worse when he silences his opponent by fencing like an old hand also."'

'And what did they say to that?' asked the girl.

'It is painful for me to repeat it,' said Forain, 'but it is quite as uncomfortable a surprise to me. Just as I seem to have cornered them finally, that red-bearded man, Le Caron, whose sword made the mortal thrust, himself broke in like one abandoning disguise, with impatience and passion. "I respect the dead," he said, "but you force me from any reticence. I can only tell you it was not we, the elder men, who dragged the boy into drink; it was he who dragged us. He arrived at the château half drunk already, and insisted on the baron ordering champagne from the Seven Stars down the road, for we were a temperate party and the cellar was not even stocked. It was he who insisted on play; it was he who taunted us with being afraid to play; it was he who at last added, quite wantonly and in wild falsehood, the intolerable taunt that we cheated at play."'

'I will not believe it,' said Crane, but his daughter remained silent, with her pale and penetrating face turned towards the amateur detective, who continued his report of the conversation.

'Oh, I don't ask you to take my word,' Le Caron went on. 'Ask Lorraine himself, ask Dr Vandam himself, who was sent to the inn for the wine, so that he was away when the row occurred. He stopped behind there to settle, and wasn't sorry, I think, to be out of it. He also, like myself, is glad to be *bourgeois* in these matters. Ask the innkeeper himself; he will tell you the wine was brought well on in the evening, after the young man arrived. Ask the people at the railway station; they will tell you when the young man arrived. You can easily test my story.'

'I can see by your face,' said the girl in a low voice, 'that you have tested it. And you have found it true.'

'You see the heart of things,' said Forain.

'I cannot see the hearts of these men,' she answered. 'But I can see the hollows where their hearts should be.'

'You still find them horrible,' he said. 'Who can blame you?'

'Horrible!' cried the old man. 'Didn't they murder my son?'

'I speak only as an adviser,' observed the Frenchman. 'I know you cannot believe a duellist could be a respectable man. I only say that, as a fact, these seem to be respectable men. I have not only verified their tale but traced back something of their past. They seem to have been concerned with commercial things, but solidly and on a considerable scale; I am in touch with the police dossiers, and should know of any such scandals about them. Forgive me; I fear I do not think that a duel is something justifiable. I will not horrify you by saying that this one was justifiable. I only warn you that, in French opinion, they may be able to justify it.'

'Yes,' said the girl. 'They grow more horrible as you speak of them. Oh! that is the really horrible man – the man who can always be justified. Honest men leave more holes gaping, like my poor brother, but the wicked are always in armour. Is there anything so blasphemous as the bad man's case when his case is complete, as the lawyers say; when the judge gravely sums up, and the jury agree and the police obey, and everything goes on oiled wheels? Is there anything so oily as the smell of that oil? It is then that I cannot wait for the Day of Judgment to crack their whited sepulchres.'

'And it is then,' said Forain quietly, 'that I fight a duel.'

The girl started a little. 'Then?' she repeated.

'Then,' repeated the Frenchman, lifting his head. 'You, Mademoiselle, have uttered the defence of the good duellist. You have proved the right of the private gentleman to draw a private sword. Yes, it is then that I do this criminal and bloody thing that so much horrifies you and your father. Yes, it is then that I become a murderer. When there is no crack in the whitewash and I cannot wait for the wrath of God. And permit me the reminder that you have not yet heard the end of my interview with the men who have left you in mourning.'

Crane still stared in frosty suspicion, but the girl, as Forain suggested, had great intuitions. Her face and eyes kindled as she gazed.

'You don't mean – ' she began, and then stopped.

Forain rose to his feet. 'Yes,' he said. 'Being such a bloodthirsty character, I must no longer remain in company so respectable. Yes, mademoiselle, I have challenged the man who killed your brother.'

'Challenged!' repeated the bristling Crane. 'Challenged – more of this – of this butchery!' and he choked. But the girl had risen also and stretched out her hand like a queen.

'No, father,' she said. 'This gentleman is our friend, and he caught me out fairly. But I see now that there is more in French wit than we have understood; yes, and more in French duelling.'

With a heightened colour and a lowered voice. Forain answered: 'Mademoiselle, my inspiration is English.' And, with a rather abrupt bow, he strode away, accompanied by Harry Monk, who regarded him with a contained amusement.

'I cannot affect to hope,' said Monk airily, 'that I myself constitute the English inspiration of your life.'

'Nonsense,' said the other rather testily, 'let us get back to business. As I imagined your views of duelling were so similar to old Crane's that you could not consistently represent me, I've asked his unfortunate son's seconds to act as mine. I believe that young Lorraine will be of great use in helping us to probe this mystery. I have talked to him, and I am convinced of his great ability.'

'And you have talked to me for years,' said Monk, laughing, 'and you are convinced of my great stupidity.'

'Of your great sincerity,' said Forain. 'That is why I do not ask you to help me here.'

Monk's scruples, however, did not prevent his being present at the new encounter that had been so rapidly and even irregularly arranged. And his travels with his eccentric friend, which had already begun to remind him of the overturns and recurrences of a nightmare, brought him a few days later back to the old duelling ground of the Château d'Orage. The garden of Baron Bruno had apparently been selected for a second time as a sort of concession to the baron's party, but it was rather a grim privilege, and they evidently felt it as such. So little disposed were they, indeed, to linger about the place where they had once feasted and fought, that the baron's motor was waiting in the road without to take them back immediately to Paris. Forain had always vaguely felt that the baron was very tenuously attached to his house and property, and in this case his party seemed to revisit it like ghosts. The prejudice of Margaret Crane would have said that a shadow of doom was visibly closing in on them. But it was more reasonable, and consonant with the more quiet and *bourgeois* character to which they seemed entitled, to suppose that they were naturally distressed at returning to the scene of their one reluctant deed of blood. Whatever the reason, the baron's brown face was heavy and sombre, and Le Caron, when he again found himself standing sword in hand on that fatal grass, was so white that his beard looked scarlet, like false hair or fiery paint. Monk almost fancied that the bright point of the poised rapier was faintly vibrant, as in a hand that shook.

The pine-shadowed park, with its careless and almost colourless decay, seemed a place where centuries might pass unnoticed. The white morning light served only to accentuate the grey details, and Monk caught himself fancying that it was truly the ashen vegetation of primeval aeons. This may have been an effect of his nerves, which were not unnaturally strained. After all, this was the third duel in those grounds, and two had ended in death; he could not but wonder if his friend was to be the last victim. Anyhow, it seemed to him that the preliminaries were intolerably lengthy. Le Caron had long and low-voiced consultations with the lowering baron; and even Forain's own seconds, Lorraine and the doctor, seemed more inclined to wait and whisper than to come to the mortal business. And all this was the more because the fight, when it did come at last, seemed to be over in a flash, like a conjuring trick.

The swords had barely touched twice or thrice when Le Caron found himself swordless. His weapon had twitched itself like a live thing out of his hand, and went spinning and sparkling over the garden wall; they could hear the steel tinkle on the stones of the road. Forain disarmed him with a turn of the wrist.

Forain straightened himself and made a salute with his sword.

'Gentlemen,' he said, 'I am quite satisfied, if you are. After all, it was a slight cause of quarrel, and the honour of both parties is, so far, secure. Also, I understand, you gentlemen are anxious to get back to town.'

Monk had long felt that his friend was more and more disposed to let the opposite group off lightly; he had long been speaking of them soberly as sober merchants. But whether or no it was the anti-climax of safety, he had a sense that the figures opposite had shrunk, and were more commonplace and ugly. The eagle nose of Le Caron looked more like a common hook; his fine clothes seemed to sit more uneasily on him, as on a hastily dressed doll; and even the solid and solemn baron somehow looked more like a large dummy outside a tailor's shop. But the strangest thing of all was that the baron's other colleague, Valance, of the shaven head, was standing astraddle in the background, wearing a broad though a bitter grin. As the baron and the defeated duellist made their way rather sullenly through the garden door to the car beyond, Forain went up to this last member of the strange group, and (much to Monk's surprise) talked quickly and quietly for several minutes. It was only when Bruno's great voice was heard calling his name from without that this last figure also turned and left the gardens.

'*Exeunt* brigands!' said Forain with a cheerful change in his voice, 'and now the four detectives will go up and examine the brigands' den.'

And he turned and began once again to mount the slope to the château, the rest following in single file. Monk, who was just behind him, remarked abruptly when they were halfway up the ascent:

'So you didn't kill him, after all?'

'I didn't want to kill him,' replied his French friend.

'What did you want?'

'I wanted to see whether he could fence,' said Forain. 'He can't.'

Monk eyed in a puzzled manner the tall, straight, grey-clad back of the figure mounting ahead of him, but was silent till Forain spoke again.

'You remember,' continued that gentleman, 'that old Crane said his unfortunate son had actually got prizes for fencing. But that carroty-whiskered Mr Le Caron hardly knows how to hold a foil. Of course, it's very natural; after all, he is but a quiet business man, as I told you, and deals more in gold than steel.'

'But, my good man,' cried Monk, addressing the back in exasperation, 'what the devil does it all mean? Why was Crane killed in the duel?'

'There never was any duel,' said Forain, without turning round.

Dr Vandam behind uttered an abrupt sound as of astonishment, or perhaps enlightenment; but, though it was followed by many questions, Forain said no more till they stood in the long inner room of the château, with the weapons on the wall and the ebony cabinet, on which the black cherubs looked blacker than ever. Forain felt more darkly a certain contradiction between their colour and shape, that was like a blasphemy. Black cherubs were like the Black Mass – they were symbols of some idea that hell is an inverted copy of heaven, like a landscape hanging downwards in a lake.

He shook off his momentary dreams and stooped over the drawers of the cabinet, and when he spoke again it was lightly enough.

'You know the château, Monsieur Lorraine,' he said, 'and I expect you know the cabinet, and even the drawer. I see it's been opened lately.' The drawer, indeed, was not completely closed, and, giving it a sudden jerk, he pulled it completely out of the cabinet. Without further words he bore it, with its contents, back into the card-room and put it on the round table; and at his invitation his three colleagues or co-detectives drew up their chairs and sat round it. The drawer seemed to contain the contents of an old curiosity shop, such as Balzac loved to describe – a tumbled heap of brown coins, dim jewels and trinkets, of which tales, true and false, are told.

'Well, what about it?' asked Monk. 'Do you want to get something out of it?'

'Not exactly,' replied the investigator. 'I rather fancy I want to put something into it.'

He pulled from his pocket the locket with the dark portrait, and poised it thoughtfully in his hand.

'We have now to ask ourselves,' went on the detective to his colleagues, 'why young Crane was carrying this, which is a portrait of the countess?'

'He went about Paris a good deal,' said Dr Vandam, rather grimly.

'If she knew him well,' proceeded Forain, 'it seems strange she has taken no notice of his sad end.'

'Perhaps she knew him a little too well,' cried Lorraine, with a little laugh. 'Or perhaps, though it's an ugly thing to say, she was glad to be rid of him. There were uglier stories when her husband, the old count – '

'You know the château, Monsieur Lorraine?' repeated Forain, looking at him steadily and even sternly. 'I think that's where the locket came from.' And he tossed it on to the many-coloured heap in the drawer.

Lorraine's eyes were literally like black diamonds as he gazed fascinated at the heap; he seemed really too excited to reply. Forain continued his exposition.

'Poor Crane, I fancy, must have found it here. Or else somebody found it here and gave it to him. Or else somebody – by the way, surely that's a real Renascence chain there – Italian and fifteenth century, unless I'm wrong. There are valuable things here, Monsieur Lorraine, and I believe you're a judge of them.'

'I know a little about the Renascence,' answered Lorraine, and the pale Dr Vandam flashed a queer look at him through his spectacles.

'There was a ring, too, I suspect,' said Forain. 'I have put back the locket. Would you, Monsieur Lorraine, kindly put back the ring?'

Lorraine rose, the smile still on his lips; he put two fingers in his waistcoat pocket and drew out a small circlet of wrought gold with a green stone.

The next moment Forain's arm shot across the table trying to catch his wrist; but his motion, though swift as his sword-thrust, was yet too late. Young Mr Waldo Lorraine stood with the smile on his lips and the Renascence ring on his finger while one could count five. Then his feet slipped on the smooth floor and he fell dead across the table, with his black ringlets among the rich refuse of the drawer. Almost simultaneously with the shock of his fall Dr Vandam had taken one bound, burst out of the french windows and disappeared down the garden like a cat.

'Don't move,' said Forain with a steely steadiness. 'The police are on the watch. I laid them on the other day in Paris when I saw poor Crane's body.'

'But surely,' cried his bewildered friend, 'it was not only then that you saw the wound on his body.'

!I mean the wound on his finger,' said Forain.

He stood a minute or two in silence, looking down at the fallen figure across the table with pity and something almost like admiration.

'Strange,' he said at last, 'that he should die just here, with his head in all that dustbin of curiosities that he was born among and had such a taste for. You saw he was a Jew, of course, but, my God, what a genius! Like your young Disraeli – and he might have succeeded too and filled the world with his fame. Just a mistake or two, breaking a cucumber frame in the dark, and he lies dead in all that dead bric-á-brac, as if in the pawnshop where he was born.'

The next appointment Forain made with his friends was at the office of the *Sûreté* in a private room. Monk was a little late for the appointment; the party was already assembled round the table, and it gave him a final shock. He was not, indeed, surprised to see Crane and his daughter sitting opposite Forain, and he guessed that the man presiding, with the white beard and the red rosette, was the chief of police himself. But his head turned when he found the fifth place filled with the broad shoulders, cropped hair and ghastly handsome face of Valence, the youngest second of Le Caron.

Old Crane was in the middle of a speech when he entered, and was speaking with his usual smouldering and self-righteous indignation.

'I send my son to execute a deed of partnership in a good business with Miller, Moss & Hartman, one of the first firms in the civilized world, sir, with branches in America and all the colonies, as big as the Bank of England. What happens? No sooner does he set foot in your country than he gets in a dicing, drinking, duelling gang, and is butchered in a barbarous brawl with drawn swords.'

'Mr Crane,' said Forain gently, 'you will forgive me if I both contradict you and congratulate you. Given so sad a story, I give you the gladdest news a father could hear. You have wronged your son. He did not drink, he did not dice, he did not duel. He obeyed you in every particular. He devoted himself wholly to Messrs Miller, Moss & Hartman; he died in your service, and he died rather than fail you.'

The girl leaned swiftly forward, and she was pale but radiant.

'What do you mean?' she cried. 'Then who were these men with swords and hateful faces? What were they doing? Who are they?'

'I will tell you,' answered the Frenchman calmly. 'They are Messrs Miller, Moss & Hartman, one of the first firms in the civilized world, as big as the Bank of England.'

There was a silence of stupefaction on the other side of the table, and it was Forain who went on, but with a change and challenge in his voice.

'Oh, how little you rich masters of the modern world know about the modern world! What do you know about Miller, Moss and Hartman, *except* that they have branches all over the world and are as big as the Bank of England? You know they go to the ends of the earth, but where do they come from? Is there any check on businesses changing hands or men changing names? Miller may be twenty years dead, if he was ever alive. Miller may stand for Muller, or Muller for Moses. The back-doors of every business to-day are open to such newcomers, and do you ever ask from what gutters they come? And then you think your son lost if he goes into a music-hall, and you want to shut up all the taverns to keep him from bad company. Believe me, you had better shut up the banks.'

Margaret Crane was still staring with electric eyes. 'But what in the name of mercy happened?' she cried.

The investigator turned slightly in his chair and made a movement, as of somewhat sombre introduction, towards Valence, who sat looking at the table with a face like coloured stone.

'We have with us,' said Forain, 'one who knows from within the whole of this strange story. We need not trouble much about his own story. Of the five men who have played this horrible farce, he is certainly the most honest, and therefore the only one who has been in prison. It was for a crime of passion long ago, which turned him from being at worst a Lothario to being at worst an Apache. Hence these more respectable ruffians had a rope round his neck, and to-day he is not so much a traitor as a runaway. If on that hideous night he held a candle to the devil, he is no devil-worshipper; at least he has little worship for these devils.'

There was along silence, and the stony lips of the shaven Apollo curled and moved at last. 'Well,' he said, 'I won't trouble you with much about these men I had to serve. Their real names were not Lorraine, Le Caron, etc., any more than they were Miller, Moss, etc., though they went by the first in society and the second in business. Just now we need not trouble about their real names; I'm sure they never did. They were cosmopolitan moneylenders mostly; I was in their power, and they kept me as a big bully and bodyguard to save them from what they richly deserved at the hands of many ruined men. They would no more have thought of fighting a duel than of going on a crusade. I knew something of the countess, who has nothing to do with the story, except that I got them a short lease of her house. One evening Lorraine , who was the leader and the cleverest rascal in Europe, young as he was, happened to be turning over the drawer of curios, which he had taken out of the black cabinet and put on the round card-table. He found the old Italian ring, and told us it was poisoned; he knew a lot about such toys. Suddenly he made a momentary gesture covering the drawer, like a fence when he hears the police. He recovered his calm; there was no danger, but the gesture told of old times. What had produced it was a man who had appeared silently, and was standing outside the french windows, having entered up the garden slope. He was a slim, fair young man, carefully dressed and wearing a silk hat, which he took off as he entered. "My name is Crane," he said a little stiffly and nervously, and plucked off his glove to offer his hand, which Lorraine shook with great warmth. The others joined in the greeting, and it gradually became apparent that this was the representative of some firm with whom they were to make an important amalgamation. In the entrance-room all was welcome and gaiety, but when young Crane had followed Bruno into the big inner room, leaving his hat and gloves on the card-table by the curios, I fancy things did not go smoothly. I did not understand the business fully, but I was watching the three others who did, and I came to the conclusion that Bruno, in their name, was making some proposition to the new junior partner which they regarded as a very handsome proposition for him, but which he did not regard as altogether handsome in other respects. They seemed quite confident at first, but as the talk went on in the inner room Vandam and Le Caron exchanged gloomy glances; and suddenly a full, indignant voice came from within: "Do you mean, sir, that my father is to suffer?" and then, after an inaudible reply, "Confidential, sir! The confidence, I imagine, is placed by my father in me. I shall instantly report this astounding proposal . . . No, sir, I am not to be bribed." I was watching Lorraine's face, that seemed to have grown old as a yellow parchment, and his eyes glittered like the old stones on the table. He was leaning across it, his mouth close to the ear of Vandam, and he was saying: "He must not leave the house. Our work all over the world is lost if he leaves the house." "But we can't stop him," whispered the doctor, and his teeth chattered. "Can't!" repeated Lorraine, with a ghastly smile, yet somehow like a man in a trance: "Oh, one *can* do anything. I never did it before, though." He picked the poison ring out of the heap. Then he swiftly drew the young man's glove out of his top hat on the table. There came a burst of speech from the inner room: "I shall tell him you are a pack of thieves!" and Lorraine quietly slipped the ring inside a finger of the glove, a moment before its owner swung into the room. He clapped on his hat, furiously pulled on his gloves, and strode to the french windows. Then he flung them open wide upon the sunset, stepped out and fell dead on the garden turf beyond. I remember his tall hat rolling down the slope, and how horrible it seemed that it should still be moving among the bushes, when he lay so still."

'He died like a soldier for a flag,' said Forain.

'Perhaps you have already guessed,' went on Valence, 'the rest of the story. Hell itself must have inspired Lorraine that night, for the whole drama was his and worked out to the last detail. The difficulty in every murder is how to hide the corpse. He decided not to hide it, but to show it: I might say to advertise it. He had been striding up and down the inner hall, his flexible face working with thought, when his eye caught the crossed swords on the trophy. 'This man died in a duel,' he said. 'In England he'd have died out duck-shooting, and in Russia of dynamite. In France he died in a duel. If we all take the lighter blame, they will never look for heavier; it's a good rule with confessions,' and again he wore that awful smile. He not only staged the duel, but the drunken quarrel that was to explain it. They were quite right when they said the champagne was not sent for till after the boy's arrival. It was not sent for till after the boy's arrival. It was not sent for till after his death. They carefully scattered cards, carefully threw furniture about and so on. By the way, they didn't shuffle the packs enough to deceive Monsieur Forain. They then put Le Caron – the showiest – in his shirt-sleeves, did the same with dead man, and then Lorraine deliberately passed the sword through the heart that had already ceased to beat. It seemed like a second murder, and a worse one. Then they carried him down in the dark, just before the dawn, so that no one could possibly see him save on the fighting ground. Lorraine thought of twenty little things; he took an old miniature of the countess from the cabinet and put it in the dead man's pocket, to put people off the scent – as it did. He left Mr Crane's letter, because its warning against dissipation actually supported the story. It was all well fitted together, and if Le Caron hadn't put his foot on a cucumber-frame in the dark I doubt if even Monsieur Forain would ever have found a hole in the business.'

Margaret Crane walked firmly out of the offices of the *Sûreté*, but at the top of the steps outside she wavered and might almost have fallen. Forain caught her by the elbow, and they looked at each other for a space; then they went down the steps and down the street together. She had lost a brother in that black adventure, and what else she gained is no part of the tale of the five strange men, or, as she came to call it afterwards, the five of swords. Margaret asked one more question about it, and their talk afterwards was of deeply different matters. She only said: 'Was it the wound you discovered on his finger that made you certain?'

'Partly his finger,' he assented gravely, 'and partly his face. There was something still fresh on his face that made me fancy already that he was no waster, but had died more than worthily. It was something young and yet nobler than youth, and more beautiful than beauty. It was something I had seen somewhere else. In fact, he was the converse, so to speak, of the case in Rostand's play, *'Monsieur de Bergerac, je suis ta cousine.'*

'I don't understand you,' she said.

'It was a family likeness,' replied her companion.

3

THE NOTICEABLE CONDUCT OF PROFESSOR CHADD

Basil Grant had comparatively few friends besides myself; yet he was the reverse of an unsociable man. He would talk to any one anywhere, and talk not only well but with perfectly genuine concern and enthusiasm for that person's affairs. He went through the world, as if it were, as if he were always on the top of an omnibus or waiting for a train. Most of these chance acquaintances, of course, vanished into darkness out of his life. A few here and there got hooked on to him, so to speak, and became his lifelong intimates, but there was an accidental look about all of them as if they were windfalls, samples taken at random, goods fallen from a goods train or presents fished out of a bran-pie. One would be, let us say, a veterinary surgeon with the appearance of a jockey; another, a mild prebendary with a white beard and vague views; another a young captain in the Lancers, seemingly exactly like other captains in the Lancers; another, a small dentist from Fulham, in all reasonable certainly precisely like every other dentist from Fulham. Major Brown, small, dry, and dapper, was one of these; Basil had made his acquaintance over a discussion in a hotel cloak-room about the right hat, a discussion which reduced the little major almost to a kind of masculine hysterics, the compound of the selfishness of an old bachelor and the scrupulosity of an old maid. They had gone home in a cab together and then dined with each other twice a week until they died. I myself was another. I had met Grant while he was still a judge, on the balcony of the National Liberal Club, and exchanged a few words about the weather. Then we had talked for about half an hour about politics and God; for men always talk about the most important things to total strangers. It is because in the total stranger we perceive man himself; the image of God is not disguised by resemblances to an uncle or doubts of the wisdom of a moustache.

One of the most interesting of Basil's motley group of acquaintances was Professor Chadd. He was known to the ethnological world (which is a very interesting world, but a long way off this one) as the second greatest, if not the greatest, authority on the relations of savages to language. He was known to the neighbourhood of Hart Street, Bloomsbury, as a bearded man with a bald head, spectacles, and a patient face, the face of an unaccountable Nonconformist who had forgotten how to be angry. He went to and fro between the British Museum and a selection of blameless tea-shops, with an armful of books and a poor but honest umbrella. He was never seen without the books and the umbrella, and was supposed (by the lighter wits of the Persian MS room) to go to bed with them in his little brick villa in the neighbourhood of Shepherd's Bush. There he lived with three sisters, ladies of solid goodness, but sinister demeanour. His life was happy, as are almost all the lives of methodical students, but one would not have called it exhilarating. His only hours of exhilaration occurred when his friend Basil Grant came into the house, late at night, a tornado of conversation.

Basil, though close on sixty, had moods of boisterous babyishness, and these seemed for some reason or other to descend upon him, particularly in the house of his studious and almost dingy friend. I can remember vividly (for I was acquainted with both parties and often dined with them) the gaiety of Grant on that particular evening when the strange calamity fell upon the professor. Professor Chadd was, like most of his particular class and type (the class that is at once academic and middle-class), a Radical of a solemn and old-fashioned type. Grant was a Radical himself, but he was that more discriminating and not uncommon type of Radical who passes most of his time in abusing the Radical party. Chadd had just contributed to a magazine an article called 'Zulu Interests and the New Makango Frontier,' in which a precise scientific report of his study of the customs of the people of T'Chaka was reinforced by a severe protest against certain interference with these customs both by the British and the Germans. He was sitting with the magazine in front of him, the lamplight shining on his spectacles, a wrinkle in his forehead, not of anger, but of perplexity, as Basil Grant strode up and down the room, shaking it with his voice, with his high spirits and his heavy tread.

'It's not your opinions that I object to, my esteemed Chadd,' he was saying, 'It's you. You are quite right to champion the Zulus, but for all that you do not sympathise with them. No doubt you know the Zulu way of cooking tomatoes and the Zulu prayer before blowing one's nose; but for all that you don't understand them as well as I do, who don't know an assegai from an alligator. You are more learned, Chadd, but I am more Zulu. Why is it that the jolly old barbarians of this earth are always championed by people who are their antithesis? Why is it? You are sagacious, you are benevolent, you are well informed, but, Chadd, you are not a savage. Live no longer under that rosy illusion. Look in the glass. Ask your sisters. Consult the librarian of the British Museum. Look at this umbrella.' And he held up that sad but still respectable article. 'Look at it. For ten mortal years to my certain knowledge you have carried that object under your arm, and I have no sort of doubt that you carried it at the age of eight months, and it never occurred to you to give one wild yell and hurl it like a javelin – thus – '

And he sent the umbrella whizzing past the professor's head, so that it knocked over a pile of books with a crash and left a vase rocking.

Professor Chadd appeared totally unmoved, with his face still lifted to the lamp and the wrinkle cut in his forehead.

'Your mental processes,' he said, 'always go a little too fast. And they are stated without method. There is no kind of inconsistency' – and no words can convey the time he took to get to the end of the word – 'between valuing the right of the aborigines to adhere to their stage in the evolutionary process, so long as they find it congenial and requisite to do so. There is, I say, no inconsistency between this concession which I have just described to you and the view that the evolutionary stage in question is, nevertheless, so far as we can form any estimate of values of cosmic processes, definable in some degree as an inferior evolutionary stage.'

Nothing but his lips had moved as he spoke, and his glasses still shone like two pallid moons.

Grant was shaking with laughter as he watched him.

'True,' he said, 'there is no inconsistency, my son of the red spear. But there is a great deal of incompatibility of temper. I am very far from being certain that the Zulu is on an inferior evolutionary stage, whatever the blazes that may mean. I do not think there is anything stupid or ignorant about howling at the moon or being afraid of devils in the dark. It seems to me perfectly philosophical. Why should a man be thought a sort of idiot because he feels the mystery and peril of existence itself? Suppose, my dear Chadd, suppose it is we who are the idiots because we are not afraid of devils in the dark?'

Professor Chadd slit open a page of the magazine with a bone paper-knife and the intent reverence of the bibliophile.

'Beyond all question,' he said, 'it is a tenable hypothesis. I allude to the hypothesis which I understand you to entertain, that our civilisation is not or may not be an advance upon, and indeed (if I apprehend you) is, or may be a retrogression from states identical with or analogous to the state of the Zulus. Moreover, I shall be inclined to concede that such a proposition is of the nature, in some degree at least, of a primary proposition, and cannot adequately be argued, in the same sense, I mean, that the primary proposition of pessimism, or the primary proposition of the non-existence of matter, cannot adequately be argued. But I do not conceive you to be under the impression that you have demonstrated anything more concerning this proposition than that it is tenable, which, after all, amounts to little more than the statement that it is not a contradiction in terms.'

Basil threw a book at his head and took out a cigar.

'You don't understand,' he said, 'but, on the other hand,

as a compensation, you don't mind smoking. Why you don't object to that disgustingly barbaric rite I can't think. I can only say that I began it when I began to be a Zulu, about the age of ten. What I maintained was that although you knew more about Zulus in the sense that you are a scientist, I know more about them in the sense that I am a savage. For instance, your theory of the origin of language, something about its having come from the formulated secret language of some individual creature, though you knocked me silly with facts and scholarship in its favour, still does not convince me, because I have a feeling that that is not the way that things happen. If you ask me why I think so I can only answer that I am a Zulu; and if you ask me (as you most certainly will) what is my definition of a Zulu; I can answer that also. He is one who has climbed a Sussex apple-tree at seven and been afraid of a ghost in an English lane.'

'Your process of thought – ' began the immovable Chadd, but his speech was interrupted. His sister, with that masculinity which always in such families concentrates in sisters, flung open the door with a rigid arm and said:

'James, Mr Bingham of the British Museum wants to see you again.'

The philosopher rose with a dazed look, which always indicates in such men the fact that they regard philosophy as a familiar thing, but practical life as a weird and unnerving vision, and walked dubiously out of the room.

'I hope you do not mind my being aware of it, Miss Chadd,' said Basil Grant, 'but I hear that the British Museum has recognised one of the men who have deserved well of their commonwealth. It is true, is it not, that Professor Chadd is likely to be made keeper of Asiatic manuscripts?'

The grim face of the spinster betrayed a great deal of pleasure and a great deal of pathos also. 'I believe it's true,' she said. 'If it is, it will not only be great glory which women, I assure you, feel a great deal, but great relief, which they feel more; relief from worry from a lot of things. James's health has never been good, and while we are as poor as we are he had to do journalism and coaching, in addition to his own dreadful grinding notions and discoveries, which he loves more than man, woman, or child. I have often been afraid that unless something of this kind occurred we should really have to be careful of his brain. But I believe it is practically settled.'

'I am delighted,' began Basil, but with a worried face, 'but these red-tape negotiations are so terribly chancy that I really can't advise you to build on hope, only to be hurled down into bitterness. I've known men, and good men like your brother, come nearer than this and be disappointed. Of course, if it is true – '

'If it is true,' said the woman fiercely, 'it means that people who have never lived may make an attempt at living.'

Even as she spoke the professor came into the room with the mazed look in his eyes. 'Is it true?' asked Basil, with burning eyes.

'Not a bit true,' answered Chadd after a moment's bewilderment. 'Your argument was in three points fallacious.'

'What do you mean?' demanded Grant.

'Well,' said the professor slowly, 'in saying that you could possess a knowledge of the essence of Zulu life distinct from – '

'Oh! confound Zulu life,' cried Grant, with a burst of laughter. 'I mean, have you got the post?'

'You mean the post of keeper of the Asiatic manuscripts,' he said, opening his eye with childlike wonder. 'Oh, yes, I got that. But the real objection to your argument, which has only, I admit, occurred to me since I have been out of the room, is that it does not merely presuppose a Zulu truth apart from the facts, but infers that the discovery of it is absolutely impeded by the facts.'

'I am crushed,' said Basil, and sat down to laugh, while the professor's sister retired to her room, possibly to laugh, possibly not.

It was extremely late when we left the Chadds, and it is an extremely long and tiresome journey from Shepherd's Bush to Lambeth. This may be our excuse for the fact that we (for I was stopping the night with Grant) got down to breakfast next day at a time inexpressibly criminal, a time, in point of fact, close upon noon. Even to that belated meal we came in a very lounging and leisurely fashion. Grant, in particular, seemed so dreamy at table that he scarcely saw the pile of letters by his plate, and I doubt if he would have opened any of them if there had not lain on the top that one thing which had succeeded amid modern carelessness in being really urgent and coercive – a telegram. This he opened with the same heavy distraction with which he broke his egg and drank his tea. When he read it he did not stir a hair or say a word, but something, I know not what, made me feel that the motionless figure had been pulled together suddenly as strings are tightened on a slack guitar. Though he said nothing and did not move, I knew that he had been for an instant cleared and sharpened with a shock of cold water. It was scarcely any surprise to me when a man had drifted sullenly to his seat and fallen into it, kicked it away like a cur from under him and came round to me in two strides.

'What do you make of that?' he said, and flattened out the wire in front of me.

It ran: 'Please come at once. James's mental state dangerous. Chadd.'

'What does the woman mean?' I said after a pause, irritably. 'Those women have been saying that the poor old professor was mad ever since he was born.'

'You are mistaken,' said Grant composedly. 'It is true that all sensible women think all studious men mad. It is true, for the matter of that, all women of any kind think all men of any kind mad. But they don't put in telegrams, any more than they wire to you that grass is green or God all-merciful. These things are truisms, and often private ones at that. If Miss Chadd has written down under the eye of a strange woman in a post-office that her brother is off his head you may be perfectly certain that she did it because it was a matter of life and death, and she can think of no other way of forcing us to come promptly.'

'It will force us of course,' I said, smiling.

'Oh, yes,' he replied; 'there is a cab-rank near.'

Basil scarcely said a word as we drove across Westminster

Bridge, through Trafalgar Square, along Piccadilly, and up the Uxbridge Road. Only as he was opening the gate he spoke.

'I think you may take my word for it, my friend,' he said; 'this is one of the most queer and complicated and astounding incidents that ever happened in London or, for that matter, in any high civilisation.'

'I confess with the greatest sympathy and reverence that I don't quite see it,' I said. 'It is so very extraordinary or complicated that a dreamy somnambulant old invalid who has always walked on the borders of the inconceivable should go mad under the shock of great joy? Is it so very extraordinary that a man with a head like a turnip and a soul like a spider's web should not find his strength equal to a confounding change of fortunes? Is it, in short, so very extraordinary that James Chadd should lose his wits from excitement?'

'It would not be extraordinary in the least,' answered Basil, with placidity. 'It would not be extraordinary in the least,' he repeated, 'if the professor had gone mad. That was not the extraordinary circumstances to which I referred.'

'What,' I asked, stamping my foot, 'was the extraordinary thing?'

'The extraordinary thing,' said Basil, ringing the bell, 'is that he has not gone mad from excitement.'

The tall and angular figure of the eldest Miss Chadd blocked the doorway as the door opened. Two other Miss Chadds seemed in the same way to be blocking the narrow passage and the little parlour. There was a general sense of their keeping something from view. They seemed like three black-clad ladies in some strange play of Maeterlinck, veiling the catastrophe from the audience in the manner of the Greek chorus.

'Sit down, won't you?' said one of them, in a voice that was somewhat rigid with pain. 'I think you had better be told first what has happened.'

Then, with her bleak face looking unmeaningly out of the window, she continued, in an even and mechanical voice:

'I had better state everything that occurred just as it occurred. This morning I was clearing away the breakfast things, my sisters were both somewhat unwell, and had not come down. My brother had just gone out of the room, I believe, to fetch a book. He came back again, however, without it, and stood for some time staring at the empty grate. I said, 'Were you looking for anything I could get?' He did not answer, but this constantly happens, as he is often very abstracted. I repeated my question, and still he did not answer. Sometimes he is so wrapped up in his studies that nothing but a touch on the shoulder would make him aware of one's presence, so I came round the table towards him. I really do not know how to describe the sensation which I then had. It seems simply silly, but at the moment it seemed something enormous, upsetting one's brain. The fact is, James was standing on one leg.'

Grant smiled slowly and rubbed his hands with a kind of care.

'Standing on one leg?' I repeated.

'Yes,' replied the dead voice of the woman, without an inflection to suggest that she felt the fantasticality of her statement. 'He was standing on the left leg and had the right drawn up at a sharp angle, the toe pointing downwards. I asked him if his leg hurt him. His only answer was to shoot the leg straight at right angles to the other, as if pointing to the other with his toe to the wall. He was still looking quite gravely at the fireplace.

"James, what is the matter?" I cried, for I was thoroughly frightened. James gave three kicks in the air with the right leg, flung up the other, gave three kicks in the air with it also and spun round like a teetotum the other way. "Are you mad?" I cried. "Why don't you answer me?" He had come to a standstill, facing me, and was looking at me as he always does, with his lifted eyebrows and great spectacled eyes. When I had spoken he remained a second or two motionless, and then his only reply was to lift his left foot slowly from the floor and describe circles with it in the air. I rushed to the door and shouted for Christina. I will not dwell on the dreadful hours that followed. All three of us talked to him, implored him to speak to us with appeals that might have brought back the dead, but he has done nothing but hop and dance and kick with a solemn silent face. It looks as if his legs belonged to some one else or were possessed by devils. He has never spoken to us from that time to this.'

'Where is he now?' I said, getting up in some agitation. 'We ought not to leave him alone.'

'Doctor Colman is with him,' said Miss Chadd calmly. 'They are in the garden. Doctor Colman thought the air would do him good. And he can scarcely go into the street.'

Basil and I walked rapidly to the window which looked out on the garden. It was a small and somewhat snug suburban garden; the flower beds a little too neat and like the pattern of a coloured carpet; but on this shining and opulent summer day even they had the exuberance of something natural, I had almost said tropical. In the middle of a bright and verdant but painfully circular lawn stood two figures. One of them was a small, sharp-looking man with black whiskers and a very polished hat (I presume Dr Colman), who was talking very quietly and clearly, yet with a nervous twitch, as it were, in his face. The other was our old friend, listening with his old forbearing expression and owlish eyes, the strong sunlight gleaming on his glasses as the lamplight had gleamed the night before, when the boisterous Basil had rallied him on his studious decorum. But for one thing the figure of this morning might have been the identical figure of last night. That one thing was that while the face listened reposefully the legs were industriously dancing like the legs of a marionette. The neat flowers and the sunny glitter of the garden lent an indescribable sharpness and the incredibility to the prodigy – the prodigy of the head of a hermit and the legs of a harlequin. For miracles should always happen in broad daylight. The night makes them credible and therefore commonplace.

The second sister had by this time entered the room and came somewhat drearily to the window.

'You know, Adelaide,' she said, 'that Mr Bingham from the Museum is coming again at three.'

'I know,' said Adelaide Chadd bitterly. 'I suppose we shall

have to tell him about this. I thought that no good fortune would ever come easily to us.'

Grant suddenly turned round. 'What do you mean?' he said. 'What will you have to tell Mr Bingham?'

'You know what I shall have to tell him,' said the professor's sister, almost fiercely. 'I don't know that we need give it its wretched name. Do you think that the keeper of Asiatic manuscripts will be allowed to go on like that?' And she pointed for an instant at the figure in the garden, the shining, listening face and the unresting feet.

Basil Grant took out his watch with an abrupt movement. 'When did you say the British Museum man was coming?' he said.

'Three o'clock,' said Miss Chadd briefly.

'Then I have an hour before me,' said Grant, and without another word threw up the window and jumped out into the garden. He did not walk straight up to the doctor and lunatic, but strolling round the garden path drew near them cautiously and yet apparently carelessly. He stood a couple of feet off them, seemingly counting halfpence out of his trousers pocket, but, as I could see, looking up steadily under the broad brim of his hat.

Suddenly he stepped up to Professor Chadd's elbow, and said, in a loud familiar voice, 'Well, my boy, do you still think the Zulus our inferiors?'

The doctor knitted his brows and looked anxious, seemingly to be about to speak. The professor turned his bald and placid head towards Grant in a friendly manner, but made no answer, idly flinging his left leg about.

'Have you converted Dr Colman to your views?' Basil continued, still in the same loud and lucid tone.

Chadd only shuffled his feet and kicked a little with the other leg, his expression still benevolent and inquiring. The doctor cut in rather sharply. 'Shall we go inside, professor?' he said. 'Now you have shown me the garden. A beautiful garden. A most beautiful garden. Let us go in,' and he tried to draw the kicking ethnologist by the elbow, at the same time whispering to Grant: 'I must ask you not to trouble him with questions. Most risky. He must be soothed.'

Basil answered in the same tone, with great coolness:

'Of course your directions must be followed out, doctor. I will endeavour to do so, but I hope it will not be inconsistent with them if you will leave me alone with my poor friend in this garden for an hour. I want to watch him. I assure you, Dr Colman, that I shall say very little to him, and that little shall be as soothing as – as syrup.'

The doctor wiped his eyeglass thoughtfully.

'It is rather dangerous for him,' he said, 'to be in this strong sun without his hat. With his bald head, too.'

'That is soon settled,' said Basil composedly, and took off his own big hat and clapped it on the egglike skull of the professor. The latter did not turn round but danced away with his eyes on the horizon.

The doctor put on his glasses again, looked severely at the two for some seconds, with his head on one side, like a bird's and then saying, shortly, 'All right,' strutted away into the house, where the three Misses Chadd were all looking out from the parlour window on to the garden. They looked out on it with hungry eyes for a full hour without moving, and they saw a sight which was more extraordinary than madness itself.

Basil Grant addressed a few questions to the madman, without succeeding in making him do anything but continue to caper, and when he had done this slowly took a red note-book out of one pocket and a large pencil out of another.

He began hurriedly to scribble notes. When the lunatic skipped away from him he would walk a few yards in pursuit, stop, and make notes again. Thus they followed each other round and round the foolish circle of turf, the one writing in pencil with the face of a man working out a problem, the other leaping and playing like a child.

After about three-quarters of an hour of this imbecile scene, Grant put the pencil in his pocket, but kept the note-book open in his hand, and walking round the mad professor, planted himself directly in front of him.

Then occurred something that even those already used to that wild morning had not anticipated or dreamed. The professor, on finding Basil in front of him, stared with a blank benignity for a few seconds, and then drew up his left leg and hung it bent in the attitude that his sister had described as being the first of all his antics. And the moment he had done it Basil Grant lifted his own leg and held it out rigid before him, confronting Chadd with the flat sole of his boot. The professor dropped his bent leg, and swinging his weight on to it kicked out the other behind, like a man swimming. Basil crossed his feet like a Saltire cross, and then flung them apart again, giving a leap into the air. Then before any of the spectators could say a word or even entertain a thought about the matter, both of them were dancing a sort of jig or hornpipe opposite each other; and the sun shone down on two madmen instead of one.

They were so stricken with the deafness and blindness of monomania that they did not see the eldest Miss Chadd come out feverishly into the garden with gestures of entreaty, a gentleman following her. Professor Chadd was in the wildest posture of a *pas-de-quatre*. Basil Grant seemed about to turn a cartwheel, when they were frozen in their follies by the steely voice of Adelaide Chadd saying, 'Mr Bingham, of the British Museum.'

Mr Bingham was a slim, well-clad gentleman with a pointed and slightly effeminate grey beard, unimpeachable gloves, and formal but agreeable manners. He was the type of the over-civilised, as Professor Chadd was of the uncivilised pedant. His formality and agreeableness did him some credit under the circumstances. He had a vast experience of books and a considerable experience of the more dilettante fashionable salons. But neither branch of knowledge had accustomed him to the spectacle of two grey-haired middle-class gentlemen in modern costume throwing themselves about like acrobats as a substitute for an after-dinner nap.

The professor continued his antics with perfect placidity, but Grant stopped abruptly. The doctor had reappeared on the scene, and his shiny black eyes, under his shiny black hat, moved restlessly from one of them to the other.

'Dr Colman,' said Basil, turning to him, 'will you entertain Professor Chadd again for a little while? I am sure that he needs you. Mr Bingham, might I have the pleasure of few moments' private conversation? My name is Grant.'

Mr Bingham, of the British Museum, bowed in a manner that was respectful but a trifle bewildered.

'Miss Chadd will excuse me,' continued Basil easily, 'if I know my way about the house.' And he led the dazed librarian rapidly through the back door into the parlour.

'Mr Bingham,' said Basil, setting a chair for him, 'I imagine that Miss Chadd has told you of this distressing occurrence.'

'She has, Mr Grant,' said Bingham, looking at the table with a sort of compassionate nervousness. 'I am more pained than I can say by this dreadful calamity. It seems quite heart-rending that the thing should have happened just as we have decided to give your eminent friend a position which falls far short of his merits. As it is, of course – really, I don't know what to say. Professor Chadd may, of course, retain – I sincerely trust he will – his extraordinary valuable intellect. But I am afraid – I am really afraid – that it would not do to have the curator of the Asiatic manuscripts – er – dancing about.'

'I have a suggestion to make,' said Basil, and sat down abruptly in his chair, drawing it up to the table.

'I am delighted, of course,' said the gentleman from the British Museum. coughing and drawing up his chair also.

The clock on the mantelpiece ticked for just the moments required for Basil to clear his throat and collect his words, and then he said:

'My proposal is this. I do not know that in the strict use of words you could altogether call it a compromise, still it has something of that character. My proposal is that the Government (acting, as I presume, through your Museum) should pay Professor Chadd £800 a year until he stops dancing.'

'Eight hundred a year!' said Mr Bingham, and for the first time lifted his mild blue eyes to those of his interlocuter – and he raised them with a mild blue stare. 'I think I have not quite understood you. Did I understand you to say that Professor

Chadd ought to be employed, in his present state, in the Asiatic manuscript department at eight hundred a year?'

Grant shook his head resolutely.

'No,' he said firmly. 'No. Chadd is a friend of mine, and I would say anything for him I could. But I do not say, I cannot say, that he ought to take on the Asiatic manuscripts. I do not go so far as that. I merely say that until he stops dancing you ought to pay him £800. Surely you have some general fund for the endowment of research,'

Mr Bingham looked bewildered.

'I really don't know,' he said, blinking his eyes, 'what you are talking about. Do you ask us to give this obvious lunatic nearly a thousand a year for life?'

'Not at all,' cried Basil, keenly and triumphantly. 'I never said for life. Not at all.'

'What for then?' asked the meek Bingham, suppressing an instinct meekly to tear his hair. 'How long is this endowment to run? Not till his death? Till the Judgment day?'

'No,' said Basil, beaming, 'but just what I said. Till he has stopped dancing.' And he lay back with satisfaction and his hands in his pockets.

Bingham had by this time fastened his eyes keenly on Basil Grant and kept them there.

'Come, Mr Grant,' he said. 'Do I seriously understand you to suggest that the Government pay Professor Chadd an extraordinary high salary simply on the ground that he has (pardon the phrase) gone mad? That he should be paid more than four good clerks solely on the ground that he is flinging his boots about in the back yard?'

'Precisely,' said Grant, composedly.

'That this absurd payment is not only to run on with the absurd dancing, but actually to stop with the absurd dancing?'

'One must stop somewhere,' said Grant. 'Of course.'

Bingham rose and took up his perfect stick and gloves.

'There is really nothing more to be said, Mr Grant,' he said coldly. 'What you are trying to explain to me may be a joke – a slightly unfeeling joke. It may be your sincere view, in which case I ask your pardon for the former suggestion. But, in any case, it appears quite irrelevant to my duties. The mental morbidity, the mental downfall, of Professor Chadd, is a thing so painful to me that I cannot easily endure to speak of it. But it is clear there is a limit to everything. And if the Archangel Gabriel went mad it would sever his connection, I am sorry to say, with the British Museum Library.'

He was stepping towards the door, but Grant's hand, flung out in dramatic warning, arrested him.

'Stop!' said Basil sternly. 'Stop while there is yet time. Do you want to take part in a great work, Mr Bingham? Do you want to help in the glory of Europe – in the glory of science? Do you want to carry your head in the air when it is bald or white because of the part that you bore in a great discovery? Do you want – '

Bingham cut in sharply:

'And if I do want this, Mr Grant – '

'Then,' said Basil lightly, 'your task is easy. Get Chadd £800 a year till he stops dancing.'

With a fierce flap of his swinging gloves Bingham turned impatiently to the door, but in passing out of it found it blocked. Dr Colman was coming in.

'Forgive me. gentlemen,' he said, in a nervous, confidential voice, 'the fact is, Mr Grant, I – er – have made a most disturbing discovery about Mr Chadd.'

Bingham looked at him with grave eyes.

'I was afraid so,' he said. 'Drink, I imagine.'

'Drink!' echoed Colman, as if that were a much milder affair. 'Oh, no, it's not drink.'

Mr Bingham became somewhat agitated, and his voice grew hurried and vague. 'Homicidal mania – ' he began.

'No, no,' said the medical man impatiently.

'Thinks he's made of glass,' said Bingham feverishly. 'or says he's God – or – '

'No,' said Dr Colman sharply; 'the fact is, Mr Grant, my discovery is of a different character. The awful thing about him is – '

'Oh, go on, sir,' cried Bingham, in agony.

'The awful thing about him is,' repeated Colman, with deliberation, 'that he isn't mad.'

'Not mad!'

'There are quite well-known physical tests of lunacy,' said the doctor shortly; 'he hasn't got any of them.'

'But why does he dance?' cried the despairing Bingham. 'Why doesn't he answer us? Why hasn't he spoken to his family?'

'The devil knows,' said Dr Colman coolly. 'I'm paid to judge of lunatics, but not of fools. The man's not mad.'

'What on earth can it mean? Can't we make him listen?' said Mr Bingham. 'Can none get into any kind of communication with him?'

Grant's voice struck in sudden and clear, like a steel bell:

'I shall be very happy,' he said, 'to give him any message you like to send.'

Both men stared at him.

'Give him a message?' they cried simultaneously. 'How will you give him a message?'

Basil smiled in his slow way.

'If you really want to know how I shall give him your message,' he began, but Bingham cried:

'Of course, of course,' with a sort of frenzy.

'Well,' said Basil, 'like this.' And he suddenly sprang a foot into the air, coming down with crashing boots, and then stood on one leg.

His face was stern, though this effect was slightly spoiled by the fact that one of his feet was making wild circles in the air.

'You drive me to it,' he said. 'You drive me to betray my friend. And I will, for his own sake, betray him.'

The sensitive face of Bingham took on an extra expression of distress as of one anticipating some disgraceful disclosure. 'Anything painful, of course – ' he began.

Basil let his loose foot fall on the carpet with a crash that struck them all rigid in their feeble attitudes.

'Idiots!' he cried. 'Have you seen the man? Have you looked at James Chadd going dismally to and fro from his dingy house to your miserable library, with his futile books and his confounded umbrella, and never seen that he has the eyes of a fanatic? Have you never noticed, stuck casually behind his spectacles and above his seedy old collar, the face of a man who might have burned heretics, or died for the philosopher's stone? It is all my fault, in a way: I lit the dynamite of his deadly faith. I argued against him on the score of his famous theory about language – the theory that language was complete in certain individuals and was picked up by others simply by watching them. I also chaffed him about not understanding things in rough and ready practice. What has this glorious bigot done? He has answered me. He has worked out a system of language of his own (it would take too long to explain); he has made up, I say, a language of his own. And he has sworn that till people understand it, till he can speak to us in this language, he will not speak in any other. And he shall not. I have understood, by taking careful notice; and, by heaven, so shall the others. This shall not be blown upon. He shall finish his experiment. He shall have £800 a year from somewhere till he has stopped dancing. To stop him now is an infamous war on a great idea. It is religious persecution.'

Mr Bingham held out his hand cordially.

'I thank you, Mr Grant,' he said. 'I hope I shall be able to answer for the source of the £800, and I fancy that I shall. Will you come in my cab?'

'No, thank you very much, Mr Bingham,' said Grant heartily, 'I think I will go and have a chat with the professor in the garden.'

The conversation between Chadd and Grant appeared to be personal and friendly. They were still dancing when I left.

4

THE MODERATE MURDERER

CHAPTER I

THE MAN WITH THE GREEN UMBRELLA

The new Governor was Lord Tallboys, commonly called Top-hat Tallboys, because of his attachment to that uncanny erection, which he continued to carry balanced on his head as calmly among the palm-trees of Egypt as among the lamp-posts of Westminster. Certainly he carried it calmly enough in lands where few crowns were safe from toppling. The district he had come out to govern may here be described, with diplomatic vagueness, as a strip on the edge of Egypt and called for our convenience Polybia. It is an old story now; but one which many people had reason to remember for many years; and at the time it was an imperial event. One Governor was killed, another Governor was nearly killed; but in this story we are concerned only with one catastrophe; and that was rather a personal and even private catastrophe.

Top-hat Tallboys was a bachelor and yet he brought a family with him. He had a nephew and two nieces of whom one, as it happened, had married the Deputy Governor of Polybia, the man who had been called to rule during the interregnum after the murder of the previous ruler. The other niece was unmarried; her name was Barbara Traill; and she may well be the first figure to cross the stage of this story.

For indeed she was rather a solitary and striking figure, raven dark and rich in colouring with a very beautiful but rather sullen profile, as she crossed the sandy spaces and came under the cover of one long low wall which alone threw a strip of shadow from the sun, which was sloping towards the desert horizon. The wall itself was a quaint example of the patchwork character of that borderland of East and West. It was actually a line of little villas, built for clerks and small officials, and thrown out as by a speculative builder whose speculations spread to the ends of the earth. It was a strip of Streatham amid the ruins of Heliopolis. Such oddities are not unknown, when the oldest countries are turned into the newest colonies. But in this case the young woman, who was not without imagination, was conscious of a quite fantastic contrast. Each of these dolls' houses had its toy shrubs and plants and its narrow oblong of back garden running down to the common and continuous garden wall; and it was just outside this wall that there ran the rough path, fringed with a few hoary and wrinkled olives. Outside the fringe there faded away into infinity the monstrous solitude of sand. Only there could still be detected on that last line of distance a faint triangular shape; a sort of mathematical symbol whose unnatural simplicity has moved all poets and pilgrims for five thousand years. Any one seeing it really for the first time, as the girl did, can hardly avoid uttering a cry: 'The pyramids!'

Almost as she said it a voice said in her ear, not loud but with alarming clearness and very exact articulation: 'The foundations were traced in blood and in blood shall they be traced anew. These things are written for our instruction.'

It has been said that Barbara Traill was not without imagination; it would be truer to say that she had rather too much. But she was quite certain she had not imagined the voice; though she certainly could not imagine where it came from. She appeared to be absolutely alone on the little path which ran along the wall and led to the gardens round the Governorate. Then she remembered the wall itself, and looking sharply over her shoulder, she fancied she saw for one moment a head peering out of the shadow of a sycamore, which was the only tree of any size for some distance; since she had left the last of the low sprawling olives two hundred yards behind. Whatever it was, it had instantly vanished; and somehow she felt frightened; more frightened at its disappearance than its appearance. She began to hurry along the path to her uncle's residence at a pace that was a little like a run. It was probably through this sudden acceleration of movement that she seemed to become aware, rather abruptly, that a man was marching steadily in front of her along the same track towards the gates of the Governorate.

He was a very large man; and seemed to take up the whole of the narrow path. She had something of the sensation, with which she was already slightly acquainted, of walking behind a camel through the narrow and crooked cracks of the Eastern town. But his man planted his feet as firmly as an elephant; he walked, one might say, even with a certain pomp, as if he were in a procession. He wore a long frock-coat and his head was surmounted by a tower of scarlet, a very tall red fez, rather taller than the top-hat of Lord Tallboys. The combination of the red Eastern cap and the black Western clothes is common enough among the *Effendi* class in those countries. But somehow it seemed novel and incongruous in this case, for the man was very fair and had a big blonde beard blown about in the breeze. He might have been a model for the idiots who talk of the Nordic type of European; but somehow he did not look like an Englishman. He carried hooked on one finger a rather grotesque green umbrella or parasol, which he twirled idly like trinket. As he was walking slower and slower and Barbara was walking fast and wanted to walk faster, she could hardly repress an exclamation of impatience and something like a request for room to pass. The large man with the beard immediately faced round and stared at her; then he lifted a monocle and fixed it in his eye and instantly smiled his apologies. She realized that he must be short-sighted and that she had been a mere blur to him a moment before; but there was something else in the change of his face and manner, something that she had seen before, but to which she could not put a name.

He explained, with the most formal courtesy, that he was going to leave a note for an official at the Governorate; and there was really no reason for her to refuse him credence or conversation. They walked a little way together, talking of things in general; and she had not exchanged more than a few sentences before she realized that she was talking to a remarkable man.

We hear much in these days about the dangers of innocence; much that is false and a little that is true. But the argument is almost exclusively applied to sexual innocence. There is a great deal that ought to be said about the dangers of political innocence. That most necessary and most noble virtue of patriotism is very often brought to despair and destruction, quite needlessly and prematurely, by the folly of educating the comfortable classes in a false optimism about the record and security of the Empire. Young people like Barbara Traill have often never heard a word about the other side of the story, as it would be told by Irishmen or Indians or even French Canadians; and it is the fault of their parents and their papers if they often pass abruptly from a stupid Britishism to an equally stupid Bolshevism. The hour of Barbara Traill was come; though she probably did not know it.

'If England keeps her promises,' said the man with the beard, frowning, 'there is still a chance that things may be quiet.'

And Barbara answered, like a schoolboy:

'England always keeps her promises.'

'The Waba have not noticed,' he answered with an air of triumph.

The omniscient are often ignorant. They are often especially ignorant of ignorance. The stranger imagined that he was uttering a very crushing repartee; as perhaps he was, to any body who new what he meant. But Barbara had never heard of the Waba. The newspapers had seen to that.

'The British Government, he was saying, 'definitely pledged itself two years ago to a complete scheme of local autonomy. If it is a complete scheme, all will be well. If Lord Tallboys has come out here with an incomplete scheme, a compromise, it will very far from well. I shall be very sorry for everybody, but especially for my English friends.'

She answered with a young and innocent sneer, 'Oh yes – I suppose you are a great friend of the English.'

'Yes,' he replied calmly. 'A friend: but a candid friend.'

'Oh, I know all about that sort,' she said with hot sincerity. 'I know what they mean by a candid friend. I've always found it meant a nasty, sneering, sneaking, treacherous friend.'

He seemed stung for an instant and answered, 'Your politicians have no need to learn treachery from the Egyptians.' Then he added abruptly: 'Do you know on Lord Jaffray's raid they shot a child? Do you know anything at all? Do you even know how England tacked on Egypt to her Empire?'

'England has a glorious Empire,' said the patriot stoutly.

'England had a glorious Empire,' he said. 'So had Egypt.'

They had come, somewhat symbolically, to the end of their common path and she turned away indignantly to the gate that led into the private gardens of the Governor. As she did so he lifted his green umbrella and pointed with a momentary gesture at the dark line of the desert and the distant Pyramid. The afternoon had already reddened into evening, and the sunset lay in long bands of burning crimson across the purple desolation of that dry inland sea.

'A glorious Empire,' he said. 'An Empire on which the sun never sets. Look . . . the sun is setting in blood.'

She went through the iron gate like the wind and let it clang behind her. As she went up the avenue towards the inner garden, she lost a little of her impatient movement and began to trail along in the rather moody manner which was more normal to her. The colours and shadows of that quieter scene seemed to close about her; this place was for the present her nearest approach to home; and at the end of the long perspective of gaily coloured garden walks, she could see her sister Olive picking flowers.

The sight soothed her; but she was a little puzzled about why she should need any soothing. She had a deeply disquieting sense of having touched something alien and terrible, something fierce and utterly foreign, as if she had stroked some strange wild beast of the desert. But the gardens about her and the house beyond had already taken on a tone or tint indescribably English, in spite of the recent settlement and the African sky. And Olive was so obviously choosing flowers to put into English vases or to decorate English dinner-tables, with decanters and salted almonds.

But as she drew nearer to that distant figure, it grew more puzzling. The blossoms grasped in her sister's hand looked like mere ragged and random handfuls, torn away as a man lying on the turf would idly rear out grass, when he is abstracted or angry. A few loose stalks lay littered on the path; it seemed as if the heads had been merely broken off as if by a child. Barbara did not know why she took in these details with a slow and dazed eye, before she looked at the central figure they surrounded. Then Olive looked up and her face was ghastly. It might have been the face of Medea in the garden, gathering the poisonous flowers.

CHAPTER II

THE BOY WHO MADE A SCENE

Barbara Traill was a girl with a good deal of the boy about her. This is very commonly said about modern heroines. None the less, the present heroine would be a very disappointing modern heroine. For, unfortunately, the novelists who call their heroines boyish obviously know nothing whatever about boys. The girl they depict, whether we happen to regard her as a bright young thing or a brazen little idiot, is at any rate in every respect the complete contrary of a boy. She is sublimely candid; she is slightly shallow; she is uniformly cheerful; she is entirely unembarrassed; she is everything that a boy is not. That is, she was rather shy, obscurely imaginative, capable of intellectual friendships and at the same time of emotional brooding over them; capable of being morbid and by no means incapable of being secretive. She had that sense of misfit which embarrasses so many boys; the sense of the soul being too big to be seen or confessed, and the tendency to cover the undeveloped emotions with a convention. One effect of it was that she was of the sort troubled by Doubt. It might have been religious doubt; at the moment it was a sort of patriotic doubt; though she would have furiously denied that there was any doubt about the matter. She had been upset by her glimpse of the alleged grievances of Egypt or the alleged crimes of England; and the face of the stranger, the white face with the golden beard and the glaring monocle, had come to stand for the tempter or the spirit that denies. But the face of her sister suddenly banished all such merely political problems. It brought her back with a shock to much more private problems; indeed to much more secret problems; for she had never admitted them to anyone but herself.

The Traills had a tragedy; or rather, perhaps, something that Barbara's brooding spirit had come to regard as the dawn of a tragedy. Her younger brother was still a boy; it might more truly be said that he was still a child. His mind had never come to a normal maturity; and though opinions differed about the nature of the deficiency, she was prone in her black moods to take the darkest view and let it darken the whole house of Tallboys. Thus it happened that she said quickly, at the sight of her sister's strange expression:

'Is anything wrong about Tom?'

Olive started slightly, and then said, rather crossly than otherwise: 'No, not particularly . . . Uncle has put him with a tutor here, and they say he's getting on better . . . Why do you ask? There's nothing special the matter with him.'

'Then I suppose,' said Barbara, 'that there is something special the matter with you.'

'Well,' answered the other, 'isn't there something the matter with all of us?'

With that she turned abruptly and went back towards the house, dropping the flowers she had been making a pretence of gathering; and her sister followed, still deeply disturbed in mind.

As they came near the portico and veranda, she heard the high voice of her uncle Tallboys, who was leaning back in a garden chair and talking to Olive's husband, the Deputy Governor. Tallboys was a lean figure with a large nose and ears standing out from his stalk of a head; like many men of that type he had a prominent Adam's apple and talked in a full-throated gobbling fashion. But what he said was worth listening to; though he had a trick of balancing one clause against another, with alternate gestures of his large loose hands, which some found a trifle irritating. He was also annoyingly deaf. The Deputy Governor, Sir Harry Smythe, was an amusing contrast; a square man with a rather congested face, the colour high under the eyes, which were very light and clear, and two parallel black bars of brow and moustache; which gave him rather a look of Kitchener, until he stood up and looked stunted by the comparison. It also gave him a rather misleading look of bad temper; for he was an affectionate husband and a good-humoured comrade, if a rather stubborn party man. For the rest the conversation was enough to show that he had a military point of view, which is sufficiently common and even commonplace.

'In short,' the Governor was saying, 'I believe the Government scheme is admirably adapted to meet a somewhat difficult situation. Extremists of both types will object to it; but extremists object to everything.'

'Quite so,' answered the other; 'the question isn't so much whether they object as whether they can make themselves objectionable.'

Barbara, with her new and nervous political interests, found herself interrupted in her attempt to listen to the political conversation by the unwelcome discovery that there were other people present. There was a very beautifully dressed young gentleman, with hair like black satin, who seemed to be the local secretary of the Governor; his name was Arthur Meade. There was an old man with a very obvious chestnut wig and a very unobvious, not to say inscrutable yellow face; who was an eminent financier known by the name of Morse. There were various ladies of the official circle who were duly scattered among these gentlemen. It seemed to be the tail end of a sort of afternoon tea; which made all the more odd and suspicious the strange behaviour of the only hostess, in straying to the other garden and tearing up the flowers. Barbara found herself set down beside a pleasant old clergyman with smooth silver hair, and an equally smooth silver voice, who talked to her about the Bible and the Pyramids. She found herself committed to the highly uncomfortable experience of pretending to conduct one conversation while trying to listen to another.

This was the more difficult because the Rev. Ernest Snow, the clergyman in question, had (for all his mildness) not a little gentle pertinacity. She received a confused impression that he held very strong views on the meaning of certain Prophecies in connection with the end of the world and especially with the destiny of the British Empire. He had that habit of suddenly asking questions which is so unkind to the inattentive listener. Thus, she would manage to hear a scrap of the talk between the two rulers of the province the Governor would say, balancing his sentences with his swaying hands:

'There are two considerations and by this method we meet them both. On the one hand, it is impossible entirely to repudiate our pledge. On the other hand, it is absurd to suppose that the recent atrocious crime does not necessarily modify the nature of that pledge. We can still make sure that our proclamation is a proclamation of a reasonable liberty. We have therefore decided – '

And then, at that particular moment, the poor clergyman would pierce her consciousness with the pathetic question:

'Now how many cubits do you think that would be?'

A little while later she managed to hear Smythe, who talked much less than his companions, say curtly: 'For my part, I don't believe it makes much difference what proclamations you make. There are rows here when we haven't got sufficient forces; and there are no rows when we have got sufficient forces. That's all.'

'And what is our position at present?' asked the Governor gravely.

'Our position is damned bad, if you ask me,' grumbled the other in a low voice. 'Nothing has been done to train the men; why, I found the rifle practice consisted of a sort of parlour game with a pea-shooter about twice a year. I've put up proper rifle butts beyond the olive walk there now; but there are other things. The munitions are not –'

'But in that case,' came the mild but penetrating voice of Mr Snow, 'in that case what becomes of the Shunamites?'

Barbara had not the least idea what became of them; but in this case she felt she could treat it as a rhetorical question. She forced herself to listen a little more closely to the views of the venerable mystic; and she only heard one more fragment of the political conversation.

'Shall we really want all these military preparations?' asked Tallboys rather anxiously. 'When do you think we shall want them?'

'I can tell you,' said Smythe with a certain grimness. 'We shall want them when you publish your proclamation of reasonable liberty.'

Lord Tallboys made an abrupt movement in the garden chair, like one breaking up a conference in some irritation; then he made a diversion by lifting a finger and signalling to his secretary Mr Meade, who slid up to him and after a brief colloquy slid into the house. Released from the strain of State affairs, Barbara fell once more under the spell of the Church and the Prophetical Office. She still had only a confused idea of what the old clergyman was saying, but she began to feel a vague element of poetry in it. At least it was full of things that pleased her fancy like the dark drawings of Blake; prehistoric cities and blind and stony seers and kings who seemed clad in stone like their sepulchres the Pyramids. In a dim way she understood why all that stony and starry wilderness has been the playground of so many cranks. She softened a little towards the clerical crank and even accepted an invitation to his house on the day following, to see the documents and the definite proof about the Shunamites. But she was still very vague about what it was supposed to prove.

He thanked her and said gravely: 'If the prophecy is fulfilled now, there will be a grave calamity.'

'I suppose,' she said with a rather dreary flippancy, 'if the prophecy were not fulfilled, it would be an even greater calamity.'

Even as she spoke there was a stir behind some of the garden palms and the pale and slightly gaping face of her brother appeared above the palm-leaves. The next moment she saw just behind him the secretary and the tutor; it was evident that his uncle had sent for him. Tom Traill had the look of being too big for his clothes, which is not uncommon in the otherwise under-developed; the gloomy good looks which he would otherwise have shared with his branch of the family were marred by his dark straight hair being brushed crooked and his habit of looking out of the corner of his eye at the corner of the carpet. His tutor was a big man of a dull and dusty exterior, apparently having the name of Hume. His broad shoulders were a little bowed like those of a drudge; though he was as yet hardly middle-aged. His plain and rugged face had a rather tired expression, as well it might. Teaching the defective is not always a hilarious parlour game.

Lord Tallboys had a brief and kindly conversation with the tutor. Lord Tallboys asked a few simple questions. Lord Tallboys gave a little lecture on education; still very kindly; but accompanied by the waving of the hands in rotation. On the one hand, the power to work was a necessity of life and could never be wholly evaded. On the other hand, without a reasonable proportion of pleasure and repose even work would suffer. On the one hand . . . it was at this point that the Prophecy was apparently fulfilled and a highly regrettable Calamity occurred at the Governor's tea-party.

For the boy burst out abruptly into a sort of high gurgling crow and began to flap his hands about like the wings of a penguin; repeating over and over again, 'On the one hand. On the other hand. On the one hand. On the other hand. On the one hand. On the other hand . . . Golly!'

'Tom!' cried Olive on a sharp accent of agony and there was a ghastly silence over all the garden.

'Well,' said the tutor in a reasonable undertone, which was as clear as a bell in that stillness, 'you can't expect to have three hands, can you?'

'Three hands?' repeated the boy, and then after a long silence, 'Why, how could you?'

'One would have to be in the middle, like an elephant's trunk,' went on the tutor in the same colourless conversational tone. 'Wouldn't it be nice to have a long nose like an elephant so that you could turn it this way and that and pick up things on the breakfast table, and never let go of your knife and fork?'

'Oh, you're *mad*!' ejaculated Tom with a sort of explosion that had a queer touch of exultation.

'I'm not the only mad person in the world, old boy,' said Mr Hume.

Barbara stood staring as she listened to this extraordinary conversation in that deadly silence and that highly unsuitable social setting. The most extraordinary thing about it was that the tutor said these crazy and incongruous things with an absolutely blank face.

'Didn't I ever tell you,' he said in the same heavy and indifferent voice, 'about the clever dentist who could pull out his own teeth with his nose? I'll tell you tomorrow.'

He was still quite dull and serious; but he had done the trick. The boy was distracted from his dislike of his uncle by the absurd image, just as a child in a temper is distracted by a new toy. Tom was now only looking at the tutor and followed him everywhere with his eyes. Perhaps he was not the only member of his family who did so. For the tutor, Barbara thought, was certainly a very odd person.

There was no more political talk that day; but there was not a little political news on the next. On the following morning proclamations were posted everywhere announcing the just, reasonable and even generous compromise which His Majesty's Government was now offering as a fair and final settlement of the serious social problems of Polybia and Eastern Egypt. And on the following evening the news went through the town in one blast, like the wind of the desert, that Viscount Tallboys, Governor of Polybia, had been shot down by the last of the line of olives, at the corner of the wall.

CHAPTER III

THE MAN WHO COULD NOT HATE

Immediately after leaving the little garden party, Tom and his tutor parted for the evening; for the former lived at the Governorate, while the latter had a sort of lodge or a little bungalow higher up on the hill behind amid the taller trees. The tutor said in private what everybody had indignantly expected him to say in public; and remonstrated with the youth for his display of imitative drama.

'Well, I won't like him,' said Tom warningly, 'I'd like to kill him. His nose sticks out.'

'You can hardly expect it to stick in,' said Mr Hume mildly. 'I wonder whether there's an old story about the man whose nose stuck.'

'Is there?' demanded the other in the literal spirit of infancy.

'There may be tomorrow,' replied the tutor and began to climb the steep path to his abode.

It was a lodge built mostly of bamboo and light timber with a gallery running round outside, from which could be seen the whole district spread out like a map; the grey and green squares of the Governorate building and grounds; the path running straight under the low garden wall and parallel to the line of villas; the solitary sycamore breaking the line at one point and further along the closer rank of the olive trees, like a broken cloister, and then another gap and then the corner of the wall, beyond which spread brown slopes of desert, patched here and there with green, where the ground was being turfed as part of some new public works or the Deputy Governor's rapid reforms in military organization. The whole hung under him like a vast coloured cloud in the brief afterglow of the Egyptian sunset; then it was rapidly rolled in the purple gloom in which the strong stars stood out over his head and seemed nearer than the things on earth.

He stood for some moments on the gallery looking down on the darkening landscapes, his blunt features knotted in a frown of curious reflection. Then he went back into the room where he and his pupil had worked all day, or where he had worked to induce his pupil to consider the idea of working. It was a rather bare room and the few objects in it rather odd and varied. A few bookshelves showed very large and gaily coloured books containing the verses of Mr Edward Lear and very small and shabby books containing the verses of the principal French and Latin poets. A rack of pipes, all hanging crooked, gave the inevitable touch of the bachelor; a fishing-rod and an old double-barrelled gun leaned dusty and disused in a corner; for it was long ago that this man, in other ways so remote from the sports of his countrymen, had indulged those two hobbies, chiefly because they were unsociable. But what was perhaps most curious of all, the desk and the floor were littered with geometrical diagrams treated in a manner unusual among geometers; for the figures were adorned with absurd faces or capering legs, such as a schoolboy adds to the squares and triangles on the blackboard. But the diagrams were drawn very precisely; as if the draughtsman had an exact eye and excelled in anything depending on that organ.

John Hume sat down at his desk and began to draw more diagrams. A little later he lit a pipe, and began to study those he had drawn; but he did not leave his desk or his preoccupations. So the hours went by amid an unfathomable stillness around the hillside hermitage; until the distant strains of a more or less lively band floated up from below, as a signal that a dance at the Governorate was already in progress. He knew there was a dance that night and took no notice of it; he was not sentimental, but some of the tunes stirred almost mechanical memories. The Tallboys family was a little old-fashioned, even for this rather earlier time. They were old-fashioned in not pretending to be any more democratic than they were. Their dependents were dependents, decently treated; they did not call themselves liberal because they dragged their sycophants into society. It had therefore never crossed the mind of the secretary or the tutor that the dance at the Governorate was any concern of theirs. They were also old-fashioned in the arrangements of the dance itself; and the date must also be allowed for. The new dances had only just begun to pierce; and nobody had dreamed of the wild and varied freedom of our new fashion, by which a person has to walk about all night with the same partner to the same tune. All this sense of distance, material and moral, in the old swaying waltzes moved through his subconsciousness and must be allowed for in estimating what he suddenly looked up and saw.

It seemed for one instance as if, in rising through the mist, the tune had taken outline and colour and burst into his room with the bodily presence of a song; for the blues and greens of her patterned dress were like notes of music and her amazing face came to him like a cry; a cry out of the old youth he had lost or never known. A princess flying out of fairyland would not have seemed more impossible than the girl from that ball-room, though he knew her well enough as the younger sister of his charge; and the ball was a few hundred yards away. Her face was like a pale face burning through a dream and itself as unconscious as a dreamer's; for Barbara Traill was curiously unconscious of that mask of beauty fixed on her brooding boyish soul. She had been counted less attractive than her sisters and her sulks had marked her almost as the ugly duckling. Nothing in the solid man before her told of the shock of realization in his mind. She did not even smile. It was also characteristic of her that she blurted out what she had to say at once, almost as crudely as her brother:

'I'm afraid Tom is very rude to you,' she said. 'I'm very sorry. How do you think he is getting on?'

'I think most people would say,' he said slowly at last, 'that I ought to apologize for his schooling more than for his family. I'm sorry about his uncle; but it's always a choice of evils. Tallboys is a very distinguished man and can look after his own dignity, but I've got to look after my charge. And I know that is the right way with him. Don't you be worried about him. He's perfectly all right if you understand him; and it's only a matter of making up for lost time.'

She was listening, or not listening, with her characteristic frown of abstraction; she had taken the chair he offered her apparently without noticing it and was staring at the comical diagrams apparently without seeing them. Indeed, it might well have been supposed that she was not listening at all; for the next remark she made appeared to be about a totally different subject. But she often had a habit of thus showing fragments of her mind; and there was more plan in the jig-saw puzzle than many people understood. Anyhow, she said suddenly, without lifting her eyes from the ludicrous drawing in front of her:

'I met a man going to the Governorate today. A big man with a long fair beard and a single eyeglass. Do you know who he is? He said all sorts of horrid things against England.'

Hume got to his feet with his hands in his pockets and the expression of one about to whistle. He stared at the girl and said softly:

'Hullo! Has he turned up again? I thought there was some trouble coming. Yes, I know him – they call him Dr Gregory, but I believe he comes from Germany, though he often passes for English. He is a stormy petrel, anyhow; and wherever he goes there's a row. Some say we ought to have used him ourselves; I believe he once offered his talents to our Government. He's a very clever fellow and knows a frightful lot of the facts about these parts.'

'Do you mean,' she said sharply, 'that I'm to believe that man and all the things he said?'

'No,' said Hume. 'I shouldn't believe that man; not even if you believe all the things he said.'

'What do you mean?' she demanded.

'Frankly, I think he is a thoroughly bad egg,' said the tutor. 'He's got a pretty rotten reputation about women; I won't go into details, but he'd have gone to prison twice but for suborning perjury. I only say, whatever you may come to believe, don't believe him.'

'He dared to say that our Government broke its word,' said Barbara indignantly.

John Hume was silent. Something in his silence affected her like a strain; and she said quite irrationally:

'Oh, for the Lord's sake say something! Do you know he dared to say that somebody on Lord Jaffray's expedition shot a child? I don't mind their saying England's cold and hard and all that; I suppose that's natural prejudice. But can't we stop these wild, wicked lies?'

'Well,' replied Hume rather wearily, 'nobody can say that Jaffray is cold and hard. The excuse for the whole thing was that he was blind drunk.'

'Then I am to take the word of a liar!' she said fiercely.

'He's a liar all right,' said the tutor gloomily. 'And it's a very dangerous condition of the press and the public, when only the liars tell the truth.'

Something of a massive gravity in his grim humour for the moment overpowered her breathless resentment; and she said in a quieter tone: 'Do you believe in this demand for self-government?'

'I'm not very good at believing,' he said. 'I find it very hard to believe that these people cannot live or breathe without votes, when they lived contentedly without them for fifty centuries when they had the whole country in their own hands. A Parliament may be a good thing; a top-hat may be a good thing; your uncle certainly thinks so. We may like or dislike our top-hats. But if a wild Turk tells me he has a natural born right to a top-hat, I can't help answering: "Then why the devil didn't you make one for yourself?" '

'You don't seem to care much for the Nationalists either,' she said.

'Their politicians are often frauds; but they're not alone in that. That's why I find myself forced into an intermediate position; a sort of benevolent neutrality. It simply seems to be a choice between a lot of blasted blackguards and a lot of damned drivelling, doddering idiots. You see I'm a Moderate.'

He laughed a little for the first time; and his plain face was suddenly altered for the better. She was moved to say in a more friendly tone:

'Well, we must prevent a real outbreak. You don't want all our people murdered.'

'Only a little murdered,' he said, still smiling. 'yes, I think I should like some of them *rather* murdered. Not too much, of course; it's a question of a sense of proportion.'

'Now you're talking nonsense,' she said, 'and people in our position can't stand any nonsense. Harry says we may have to make an example.'

'I know,' he said. 'He made several examples when he was in command here, before Lord Tallboys came out. It was vigorous – very vigorous. But I think I know what would be better than making an example.'

'And what is that?'

'Setting an example,' said Hume. 'What about our own politicians?'

She said suddenly: 'Well, why don't you do something yourself?'

There was a silence. Then he drew a deep breath. 'Ah, there you have me. I can't do anything myself. I am futile; naturally and inevitably futile. I suffer from a deadly weakness.'

She felt suddenly rather frightened; she had encountered his blank empty eyes.

'I cannot hate,' he said. 'I cannot be angry.'

Something in his heavy voice seemed full of quality, like the fall of a slab of stone on a sarcophagus; she did not protest, and in her subconsciousness yawned a disappointment. She half realized the depth of her strange reliance and felt like one who had dug in the desert and found a very deep well; and found it dry.

When she went out on to the veranda the steep garden and plantation were grey in the moon; and a certain greyness spread over her own spirit; a mood of fatalism and of dull fear. For the first time she realized something of what strikes a Western eye in Eastern places as the unnaturalness of nature. The squat limbless growth of the prickly pear was not like the green growths of home, springing on light stalks to lovely flowers like butterflies captured out of air. It was more like the dead blind bubbling of some green squalid slime: a world of plants that were as plain and flat as stones. She hated the hairy surface of some of the squat and swollen trees of that grotesque garden; the tufts here and there irritated her fancy as they might have tickled her face. She felt that even the big folded flowers, if they opened, would have a foul fragrance. She had a latent sense of the savour of faint horror, lying over all as lightly as the faint moonshine. Just as it had chilled her most deeply, she looked up and saw something that was neither plant nor tree, though it hung as still in the stillness; but it had the unique horror of a human face. It was a very white face, but bearded with gold like the Greek statues of gold and ivory; and at the temples were two golden curls, that might have been the horns of Pan.

For the moment that motionless head might indeed have been that of some terminal god of gardens. But the next moment it had found legs and came to life, springing out upon the pathway behind her. She had already gone some distance from the hut and was not far from the illuminated grounds of the Governorate, whence the music swelled louder as she went. Nevertheless, she swung round and faced the other way, looking desperately at the figure she recognized. He had abandoned his red fez and black frock-coat and was clad completely in white, like many tropical trippers; but it gave him in the moonlight something of the silver touch of a spectral harlequin. As he advanced he screwed the shining disk into his eye and it revealed in a flash the faint memory that had always escaped her. His face in repose was clam and classic and might have been the stone mask of Jove rather than Pan. But the monocle gathered up his features into a sneer and seemed to draw his eyes closer together; and she suddenly saw that he was no more a German than an Englishman. And though she had no Anti-Semitic prejudice in particular, she felt somehow in that scene there was something sinister in a fair Jew, as in a white negro.

'We meet under yet a more beautiful sky,' he said; she hardly heard what else he said. Broken phrases from what she had heard recently tumbled through her mind, mere words like 'reputation' and 'prison'; and she stepped back to increase the distance, but moving in the opposite direction from which she had come. Afterwards she hardly remembered what had happened; he had said other things; he had tried to stop her; and an instantaneous impression of crushing and startling strength, like a chimpanzee, surprised her into a cry. Then she stumbled and ran; but not in the direction of the house of her own people.

Mr John Hume got out of his chair more quickly than was his wont and went to meet someone who stumbled up the stair without.

'My dear child,' he said, and put a hand on her shaking shoulder, giving and receiving a queer thrill like a dull electric shock. Then he went; moving quickly past her. He had seen something in the moonlight beyond and without descending the steps, sprang over the rail to the ground below, standing waist high in the wild and tangled vegetation. There was a screen of large leaves waving to and fro between Barbara and the rapid drama that followed; but she saw, as in flashes of moonlight, the tutor dart across the path of the figure in white and heard the shock of blows and saw a kick like a catapult. There was a wheel of silver legs like the arms of the Isle of Man; and then out of the dense depth of the lower thicket a spout of curses in a tongue that was not English, nor wholly German, but which shrieked and chattered in all the Ghettoes of the world. But one strange thing remained even in her disordered memory; that when the figure in white had risen tottering and turned to plunge down the hill, the white face and the furious gesture of malediction were turned, not towards the assailant, but towards the house of the Governor.

The tutor was frowning ponderously as he came again up the veranda steps, as if over some of his geometrical problems. She asked him rather wildly what he had done and he answered in his heavy voice:

'I hope I half killed him. You know I am in favour of half measures.'

She laughed rather hysterically and cried: 'You said you could not be angry.'

Then they suddenly became stiff and silent and it was with an almost fatuous formality that he escorted her down the slope to the very doors of the dancing-rooms. The sky behind the green pergolas of foliage was a vivid violet or some sort of blue that seemed warmer than any red; and the furry filaments of the great tree-trunks seemed like the quaint sea-beasts of childhood, which could be stroked and which unfolded their fingers. There was something upon them both beyond speech or even silence. He even went so far as to say it was a fine night.

'Yes,' she answered, 'it is a fine night'; and felt instantly as if she had betrayed some secret.

They went through the inner gardens to the gate of the vestibule, which was crowded with people in uniform and evening dress. They parted with the utmost formality; and that night neither of them slept.

CHAPTER IV

THE DETECTIVE AND THE PARSON

It was not until the following evening, as already noted, that the news came that the Governor had fallen by a shot from an unknown hand. And Barbara Traill received the news later than most of her friends; because she had departed rather abruptly that morning for a long ramble amid the ruins and plantations of palm, in the immediate neighbourhood. She took a sort of picnic basket with her, but light as was her visible luggage, it would be true to say that she went away to unpack upon a large scale. She went to unfold a sort of *impedimenta* which had accumulated in her memories; especially her memories of the night before. This sort of impetuous solitude was characteristic of her; but it had an immediate effect which was rather fortunate in her case. For the first news was the worst; and when she returned the worst had been much modified. It was first reported that her uncle was dead; then that he was dying; finally that he had only been wounded and had every prospect of recovery. She walked with her empty basket straight into the hubbub of discussion about these things; and soon found that the police operations for the discovery and pursuit of the criminal were already far advanced. The inquiry was in the hands of a hard-headed, hatchet-faced officer named Hayter, the chief of the detective force; who was being actively seconded by young Meade, the secretary of the Governor. But she was rather more surprised to find her friend the tutor in the very centre of the group, being questioned about his own recent experiences.

The next moment she felt a strange sort of surge of subconscious annoyance, as she realized the subject-matter of the questions. The questioners were Meade and Hayter; but it was significant that they had just received the news that Sir Harry Smythe, with characteristic energy, had arrested Dr Paulus Gregory, the dubious foreigner with the big beard. The tutor was being examined about his own last glimpse of that questionable public character; and Barbara felt a secret fury at finding the affair of the night before turned into a public problem of police. She felt as if she had come down in the morning to find the whole breakfast-table talking about some very intimate dream she had had in the middle of the night. For though she had carried that picture with her as she wandered among the tombs and the green thickets, she had felt it as something as much peculiar to herself as if she had had a vision in the wilderness. The bland, black-haired Mr Meade was especially insinuating in his curiosity. She told herself, in a highly unreasonable fashion, that she had always hated Arthur Meade.

'I gather,' the secretary was saying, 'that you have excellent reasons of your own for regarding this man as a dangerous character.'

'I regard him as a rotter and I always did,' replied Hume in a rather sulky and reluctant manner. 'I did have a bit of a kick up with him last night, but it didn't make any difference to my views, nor to his either, I should think.'

'It seems to me it might make a considerable difference,' persisted Meade. 'isn't it true that he went away cursing not only you but especially the Governor? And he went away down the hill towards the place where the Governor was shot. It's true he wasn't shot till a good time after, and nobody seems to have seen his assailant; but he might have hung about in the woods and then crept out along the wall at dusk.'

'Having helped himself to a gun from the gun-tree that grows wild in these woods, I suppose,' said the tutor sardonically. 'I swear he had no gun or pistol on him when I threw him into the prickly pear.'

'You seem to be making the speech for the defence,' said the secretary with a faint sneer. 'But you yourself said he was a pretty doubtful character.'

'I don't think he is in the least a doubtful character,' replied the tutor in his stolid way. 'I haven't the least doubt about him myself. I think he is a loose, lying, vicious braggart and humbug; a selfish, sensual mountebank. So I'm pretty sure that he didn't shoot the Governor, whoever else did.'

Colonel Hayter cocked a shrewd eye at the speaker and spoke himself for the first time.

'Ah – and what do you mean by that exactly?'

'I mean what I say,' answered Hume. 'it's exactly because he's that sort of rascal that he didn't commit that sort of rascality. Agitators of his type never do things themselves; they incite other people; they hold meetings and send round the hat and then vanish, to do the same thing somewhere else. It's a jolly different sort of person that's left to take the risks of playing Brutus or Charlotte Corday. But I confess there are two other little bits of evidence, which I think clear the fellow completely.'

He put two fingers in his waistcoat pocket and slowly and thoughtfully drew out a round flat piece of glass with a broken string.

'I picked this up on the spot where we struggled,' he said. 'It's Gregory's eye-glass; and if you look through it you won't see anything, except the fact that a man who wanted a lens as strong as that could see next to nothing without it. He certainly couldn't see to shoot as far as the end of the wall from the sycamore, which is whereabouts they think the shot must have been fired from.'

'There may be something in that,' said Hayter, 'though the

man might have had another glass of course. You said you had a second reason for thinking him innocent.'

'The second reason,' said Hume, 'is that Sir Harry Smythe has just arrested him.'

'What on earth do you mean?' asked Meade sharply. 'Why, you brought us the message from Sir Harry yourself.'

'I'm afraid I brought it rather imperfectly,' said the other, in a dull voice. 'It's quite true Sir Harry has arrested the doctor, but he'd arrested him before he heard of the attempt on Lord Tallboys. He had just arrested him for holding a seditious meeting five miles away at Pentapolis, at which he made an eloquent speech, which must have reached its beautiful peroration about the time when Tallboys was being shot at, here at the corner of the road.'

'Good Lord!' cried Meade, staring, 'you seem to know a lot about this business.'

The rather sullen tutor lifted his head and looked straight at the secretary with a steady but rather baffling gaze.

'Perhaps I do know a little about it,' he said. 'Anyhow, I'm quite sure Gregory's got a good alibi.'

Barbara had listened to this curious conversation with a confused and rather painful attention; but as the case against Gregory seemed to be crumbling away, a new emotion of her own began to work its way to the surface. She began to realize that she had wanted Gregory to be made responsible, not out of any particular malice towards him, but because it would explain and dispose of the whole incident; and dismiss it from her mind along with another disturbing but hardly conscious thought. Now that the criminal had again become a nameless shadow, he began to haunt her mind with dreadful hints of identity and she had spasms of fear, in which that shadowy figure was suddenly fitted with a face.

As has been already noted, Barbara Traill was a little morbid about her brother and the tradegy of the Traills. She was an omnivorous reader; she had been the sort of schoolgirl who is always found in a corner with a book. And this means generally, under modern conditions, that she read everything she could not understand some time before she ready anything that she could. Her mind was a hotch-potch of popular science about heredity and psycho-analysis; and the whole trend of her culture tended to make her pessimistic about everything. People in this mood never have any difficulty in finding reasons for their worst fears. And it was enough for her that, the very morning before her uncle was shot, he had been publicly insulted, and even crazily threatened by her brother.

That sort of psychological poison works itself deeper and deeper into the brain. Barbara's broodings branched and thickened like a dark forest; and did not stop with the thought that a dull, undeveloped schoolboy was really a maniac and a murderer. The unnatural generalizations of the books she had read pushed her further and further. If her brother, why not her sister? If her sister, why not herself? Her memory exaggerated and distorted the distracted demeanour of her sister in the flower-garden, till she could almost fancy that Olive had torn up the flowers with her teeth. As is always the case in such unbalanced worry, all sorts of accidents took on a terrible significance. Her sister had said, 'Is there not something the matter with all of us?' What could that mean but such a family curse? Hume himself had said he was not the only mad person present. What else could that mean? Even Dr Gregory had declared after talking to her, that her race was degenerate; did he mean that her family was degenerate? After all, he was a doctor, if he was a wicked one. Each of these hateful coincidences gave her a spiritual shock, so that she almost cried aloud when she thought of it. Meanwhile the rest of her mind went round and round in the iron circle of all such logic from hell. She told herself again and again that she was being morbid; and then told herself again and again that she was only morbid because she was mad. But she was not in the least mad; she was only young; and thousands of young people go through such a phase of nightmare; and nobody knows or helps.

But she was moved with a curious impulse in the search for help; and it was the same impulse that had driven her back across the moonlit glade to the wooden hut upon the hill. She was actually mounting that hill again, when she met John Hume coming down.

She poured out all her domestic terrors and suspicions in a flood, as she had poured out all her patriotic doubts and protests, with a confused confidence which rested on no defined reason or relation and yet was sure of itself.

'So there it is,' she said at the end of her impetuous monologue. 'I began by being quite sure that poor Tom had done it. But by this time I feel as if I might have done it myself.'

'Well, that's logical enough,' agreed Hume. 'It's about as sensible to say that you are guilty as that Tom is. And about as sensible as either of you.'

She attempted to explain her highly scientific guesses about heredity; and their effect was more marked. They succeeded at least in arousing this large and slow person to a sort of animation.

'Now the devil take all novelists and newspaper men who talk about what even the doctors don't understand! People abuse the old nurses for frightening children with bogies which pretty soon became a joke. What about the new nurses who let children frighten themselves with all the black bogies they are supposed to take seriously? My dear girl, there is nothing the matter with your brother, any more than with you. He's only what they call a protected neurotic; which is their long-winded way of saying he has an extra skin that the Public School varnish won't stick on, but runs off like water off a duck's back. So much the better for him, as likely as not, in the long run. But even suppose he did remain a little more like a child than the rest of us. Is there anything particularly horrible about a child? Do you shudder when you think of your dog, merely because he's happy and fond of you and yet can't do the forty-eighth proposition of Euclid? Being a dog is not a disease. Being a child is not a disease; don't you sometimes wish we could all remain children?'

She was of the sort that grapples with notions and suggestions one after another, as they come; and she stood silent; but her mind was busy like a mill. It was he who spoke again, and more lightly.

'It's like what we were saying about making examples. I think the world is much too solemn and severe about punishments; it would be far better if it were ruled like a nursery. People don't want penal servitude and execution and all the rest. What most people want is to have their ears boxed or be sent to bed. What fun it would be to take an unscrupulous millionaire and make him stand in the corner! Such an appropriate penalty!'

When she spoke again there was in her tones something of relief and a renewed curiosity.

'What do you do with Tom?' she asked, 'and what's the meaning of all those funny triangles.'

'I play the fool,' he replied gravely. 'What he wants is to have his attention aroused and fixed; obvious foolery. Don't you know how they have always liked such images as the cow jumping over the moon? It's the educational effect of riddles. Well, I have to be the riddle. I have to keep him wondering what I mean or what I shall do next. It means being an ass; but it's the only way.'

'Yes,' she answered slowly, 'there's something awfully rousing about riddles . . . all sorts of riddles. Even that old parson with his riddles out of Revelations makes you feel he has something to live for . . . by the way, I believe we promised to go to tea there this afternoon; I've been in a state to forget everything.'

Even as she spoke she saw her sister Olive coming up the path attired in the unmistakable insignia of one paying calls, and accompanied by her sturdy husband, the Deputy Governor, who did not often attend these social functions. They all went down the road together and Barbara was vaguely surprised to see ahead of them on the same road, not only the sleek and varnished figure of Mr Meade the secretary, but also the more angular outline of colonel Hayter. The clergyman's invitation had evidently been a comprehensive one.

The Rev. Ernest Snow lived in a very modest manner in one of the little houses that had been erected in a row for the minor officials of the Governorate. It was at the back of this line of villas that the path ran along the garden wall and past the sycamore to the bunch of olives and finally to the corner where the Governor had fallen by the mysterious bullet. That path fringed the open desert and had all the character of a rude beaten path for the desert pilgrims. But walking on the other side, in front of the row of houses, a traveller might well have imagined himself in any London suburb, so regular were the ornamental railings and so identical the porticoes and the small front-garden plots. Nothing but a number distinguished the house of the clergyman; and the entrance of guests from the Governorate had some difficulty in squeezing through it.

Mr Snow bowed over Olive's hand with a ceremony that seemed to make his white hair a ghost of eighteenth century powder, but also with something else that seemed at first a shade more difficult to define. It was something that went with the lowered voice and lifted hand of his profession at certain moments. His face was composed, but it would almost seem deliberately composed; and in spite of his grieved tone his eyes were very bright and steady. Barbara suddenly realized that he was conducting a funeral; and she was not far out.

'I need not tell you, Lady Smythe,' he said in the same soft accents, 'what sympathy we all feel in this terrible hour. If only from a public standpoint, the death of your distinguished uncle – '

Olive Smythe struck in with a rather wild stare.

'But my uncle isn't dead, Mr Snow. I know they said so at first; but he only got a shot in his leg and he is trying to limp about already.'

A shock of transformation passed over the clergyman's face, too quick for most eyes to follow; it seemed to Barbara that his jaw dropped and when it readjusted itself, it was in a grin of utterly artificial congratulation.

'My dear lady,' he breathed, 'for this relief – '

He looked round a little vacantly at the furniture. Whether the Rev. Ernest Snow had remembered to prepare tea at tea-time, was not yet quite clear; but the preparations he had made seemed to be of a less assuaging sort. The little tables were loaded with large books, many of them lying open; and these were mostly traced with sprawling plans and designs, mostly architectural or generally archaeological, in some cases apparently astronomical or astrological, but giving as a whole a hazy impression of a magician's spells or a library of the black art.

'Apocalyptic studies,' he stammered, 'a hobby of mine. I believed that my calculations . . . these things are written for our instruction.'

And then Barbara felt a final stab of astonishment and alarm. For two facts became instantly and simultaneously vivid to her consciousness. The first was that the Rev. Ernest Snow had been reposing upon the fact of the Governor's death with something very like a solemn satisfaction, and had heard of his recovery with something quite other than relief. And the second was that he spoke with the same voice that had once uttered the same words, out of the shadow of the sycamore, that sounded in her ears like a wild cry for blood.

CHAPTER V

THE THEORY OF MODERATE MURDER

Colonel Hayter, the Chief of the Police, was moving towards the inner rooms with a motion that was casual but not accidental. Barbara indeed had rather wondered why such an official had accompanied them on a purely social visit; and she now began to entertain dim and rather incredible possibilities. The clergyman had turned away to one of the bookstands and was turning over the leaves of a volume with feverish excitement; it seemed almost that he was muttering to himself. He was a little like a man looking up a quotation on which he has been challenged.

'I hear you have a very nice garden here, Mr. Snow,' said Hayter. 'I should rather like to look at your garden.'

Snow turned a startled face over his shoulder; he seemed at first unable to detach his mind from his preoccupation; then he said sharply but a little shakily, 'There's nothing to see in my garden; nothing at all. I was just wondering –'

'Do you mind if I have a squint at it?' asked Hayter indifferently; and shouldered his way to the back-door. There was something resolute about his action that made the others trail vaguely after him, hardly knowing what they did. Hume, who was just behind the detective, said to him in an undertone:

'What do you expect to find growing in the old man's garden?'

Hayter looked over his shoulder with a grim geniality. 'Only a particular sort of tree you were talking of lately,' he said.

But when they went out into the neat and narrow strip of back garden, the only tree in sight was the sycamore spreading over the desert path; and Barbara remembered with another subconscious thrill that this was the spot from which, as the experts calculated, the bullet had been fired.

Hayter strode across the lawn and was seen stooping over something in the tangle of tropical plants under the wall. When he straightened himself again he was seen to be holding a long and heavy cylindrical object.

'Here is something fallen from the gun-tree you said grew in these parts,' he said grimly. 'Funny that the gun should be found in Mr. Snow's back-garden, isn't it? Especially as it's a double-barrelled gun with one barrel discharged.'

Hume was staring at the big gun in the detective's hand; and for the first time his usually stolid face wore an expression of amazement and even consternation.

'Damn it all!' he said softly, 'I forgot about that. What a rotten fool I am!'

Few except Barbara even heard his strange whisper: and nobody could make any sense of it. Suddenly he swung around and addressed the whole company aloud, almost as if they were a public meeting.

'Look here,' he said, 'do you know what this means? This means that poor old Snow, who is probably still fussing over his hieroglyphics, is going to be charged with attempted murder.'

'It's a bit premature,' said Hayter, 'and some would say you were interfering in our job, Mr. Hume. But I owe you something for putting us right about the other fellow, when I admit we were wrong.'

'You were wrong about the other fellow and you are wrong about this fellow,' said Hume, frowning savagely. 'But I happened to be able to offer you evidence in the other case. What evidence can I give now?'

'Why should you have any evidence to give?' asked the other, very much puzzled.

'Well I have,' said Hume, 'and I jolly well don't want to give it.' He was silent for a moment and then broke out in a sort of fury: 'Blast it all, can't you *see* how silly it is to drag in that silly old man? Don't you see he'd only fallen in love with his own prophesies of disaster, and was a bit put off when they didn't come true after all?'

'There are a good many more suspicious circumstances,' cut in Smythe curtly. 'There's the gun in the garden and the position of the sycamore..'

There was a long silence during which Hume stood with huge hunched shoulders frowning resentfully at his boots. Then he suddenly threw up his head and spoke with a sort of explosive lightness.

'Oh, well then, I must give my evidence,' he said, with a smile that was almost gay: 'I shot the Governor myself.'

There was s stillness as if the place had been full of statues; and for a few seconds nobody moved or spoke. Then Barbara heard her own voice in the silence crying out:

'Oh, you didn't!'

A moment later the Chief of Police was speaking with a new and much more official voice:

'I should like to know whether you are joking,' he said, 'or whether you really mean to give yourself up for the attempted murder of Lord Tallboys.'

Hume held up one hand in an arresting gesture, almost like a public speaker. He was still smiling slightly, but his manner had grown more grave.

'Pardon me,.' he said. 'Pardon me. Let us distinguish. The

distinction is of great value to my self-esteem. I did not try to murder the Governor. I tried to shoot him in the leg and I did shoot him in the leg.'

'What is the sense of all this?' cried Smythe with impatience.

'I am sorry to appear punctilious,' said Hume calmly. 'Imputations on my morals I must bear, like any other members of the criminal class. But imputations on my marksmanship I cannot tolerate; it is the only sport in which I excel.' He picked up the double-barrelled gun before they could stop him and went on rapidly: 'And may I draw attention to one technical point? This gun has two barrels and one is still undischarged. If any fool had shot Tallboys at this distance and not killed him, don't you think even a fool would have shot again, if that was what he wanted to do? Only, you see, it was not what I wanted to do.'

'You seem to fancy yourself a lot as a marksman,' said the Deputy-Governor rudely.

'Ah, you are sceptical,' replied the tutor in the same airy tone. 'Well, Sir Harry, you have yourself provided the apparatus of demonstration, and it will not take a moment. The targets which we owe to your patriotic efficiency are already set up, I think, on the slope just beyond the end of the wall.' Before anybody could move he had hopped up on to the low garden wall, just under the shadow of the sycamore. From that perch he could see the long line of the butts stretching along the border of the desert.

'Suppose we say,' he said pleasantly, in the tone of a popular lecturer, 'that I put this bullet about an inch inside the white on the second target.'

The group awoke from its paralysis of surprise: Hayter ran forward and Smythe burst out with: 'Of all the damned tomfoolery – '

His sentence was drowned in the deafening explosion, and amid the echoes of it the tutor dropped serenely from the wall.

'If anybody cares to go and look,' he said, 'I think he will find the demonstration of my innocence – not indeed of shooting the Governor, but of wanting to shoot him anywhere else but where I did shoot him.'

There was another silence; and then this comedy of unexpected happenings was crowned with another that was still more unexpected; coming from the one person whom everybody had naturally forgotten.

Tom's high crowing voice was suddenly heard above the crowd.

'Who's going to look?' he cried. 'Well, why don't you go and look?'

It was almost as if a tree in the garden had spoken. And indeed the excitement of events had worked upon that vegetating brain till it unfolded rapidly, as do some vegetables at the touch of chemistry. Nor was this all; for the next moment the vegetable had taken on a highly animal energy and hurled itself across the garden. They saw a whirl of lanky limbs against the sky as Tom Traill cleared the garden wall and went plunging away through the sand towards the targets.

'Is this place a lunatic asylum?' cried Sir Harry Smythe, his face still more congested with colour and a baleful light in his eyes, as if a big but buried temper was working its way to the surface.

'Come, Mr. Hume,' said Hayter in a cooler tone, 'everybody regards you as a very sensible man. Do you mean to tell me seriously that you put a bullet in the Governor's leg for no reason at all, not even murder.'

'I did it for an excellent reason,' answered the tutor, still beaming at him in a rather baffling manner. 'I did it because I am a sensible man. In fact, I am a Moderate Murderer.'

'And what the blazes may that be?'

'The philosophy of moderation in murder,' continued the tutor blandly, 'is one to which I have given some little attention. I was saying only the other day that what most people want is to be rather murdered; especially persons in responsible political situations. As it is, the punishments on both sides are far too severe. The merest touch or *soupçon* of murder is all that is required for purposes of reform. The little more and how much it is; the little less and the Governor of Polybia gets clean away, as Browning said.'

'Do you really ask me to believe,' snorted the Chief of Police, 'that you make a practice of potting every public man in the left leg?'

'No, no,' said Hume, with a sort of hasty solemnity. 'The treatment, I assure you, is marked with much more individual attention. Had it been the Chancellor of the Exchequer, I should perhaps have selected a portion of the left ear. In the case of the Prime Minister the tip of the nose would be indicated. But the point is the general principle that *something* should happen to these people, to arouse their dormant faculties by a little personal problem. Now if ever there was a man,' he went on with delicate emphasis, as if it were a scientific demonstration, 'if ever there was a man meant and marked out by nature to be rather murdered, it is Lord Tallboys. Other eminent men, very often, are just murdered; and everyone feels that the situation has been adequately met; that the incident is terminated. One just murders them and thinks no more about it. But Tallboys is a remarkable case; he is my employer and I know him pretty well. He is a good fellow, really. He is a gentleman, he is a patriot; what is more, he is really a liberal and reasonable man. But by being perpetually in office he has let that pompous manner get worse and worse, till it seems to grow on him, like his confounded top-hat. What is needed in such a case? A few days in bed, I decided. A few healthful weeks standing on one leg and meditating on that fine shade of distinction between oneself and God Almighty, which is so easily overlooked.'

'Don't listen to any more of this rubbish,' cried the Deputy-Governor. 'If he says he shot Tallboys, we've got to take him up for it, I suppose. He ought to know.'

'You've hit it at last, Sir Harry,' said Hume heartily, 'I'm arousing a lot of dormant intellects this afternoon.'

'We won't have any more of your joking,' cried Smythe with sudden fury; 'I'm arresting you for attempted murder.'

'I know,' answered the smiling tutor, 'that's the joke.'

At this moment there was another leap and scurry by the

sycamore and the boy Tom hurled himself back into the garden, panting aloud:

'It's quite right. It's just where he said.'

For the rest of the interview, and until that strange group had broken up on the lawn, the boy continued to stare at Hume as only a boy can stare at somebody who has done something rather remarkable in a game. But as he and Barbara went back to the Governorate together, the latter indescribably dazed and bewildered, she found her companion curiously convinced of some view of his own, which he was hardly competent to describe. It was not exactly as if he disbelieved Hume or his story. It was rather as if he believed what Hume has not said, rather than what he had.

'It's a riddle,' repeated Tom with stubborn solemnity. 'He's awfully fond of riddles.; He says silly things just to make you think. That's what we've got to do. He doesn't like you to give it up.'

'What we've got to do?' repeated Barbara.

'Think what it really means,' said Tom.

There was some truth perhaps in the suggestion that Mr. John Hume was fond of riddles; for he fired off one more of them at the Chief of Police, even as that official took him into custody.

'Well,' he said cheerfully, 'you can only half hang me because I'm only half a murderer. I suppose you have hanged people sometimes?'

'Occasionally, I'm sorry to say,' replied Colonel Hayter.

'Did you ever hang somebody to prevent him being hanged?' asked the tutor with interest.

CHAPTER VI

THE THING THAT REALLY HAPPENED

It is not true that Lord Tallboys wore his top-hat in bed, during his brief indisposition. Nor is it true, as was more moderately alleged, that he sent for it as soon as he could stand upright and wore it as a finishing touch to a costume consisting of a green dressing-gown and red slippers. But it was quite true that he resumed his hat and his high official duties at the earliest possible opportunity; rather to the annoyance, it was said, of his subordinate the Deputy-Governor, who found himself for the second time checked in some of those vigorous military measures which are always more easily effected after the shock of a political outrage. In plain words, the Deputy-Governor was rather sulky. He had relapsed into a red-faced and irritable silence; and when he broke it his friends rather wished he would relapse into it again. At the mention of the eccentric tutor, whom his department had taken into custody, he exploded with a special impatience and disgust. 'Oh, for God's sake don't tell me about that beastly madman and mountebank!' he cried, almost in the voice of one tortured and unable to tolerate a moment more of human folly. 'Why in the world are we cursed with such filthy fools . . . shooting him in the leg . . . moderate murderer . . . mouldy swine!'

'He's not a mouldy swine,' said Barbara Traill emphatically, as if it were an exact point of natural history. 'I don't believe a word of what you people are saying against him.'

'Do you believe what he is saying against himself?' asked her uncle, looking at her with screwed-up eyes and a quizzical expression. Tallboys was leaning on a crutch; in marked contrast to the sullenness of Sir Harry Smythe, he carried his disablement in a very plucky and pleasant fashion. The necessity of attending to the interrupted rhythm of his legs had apparently arrested the oratorical rotation of his hands. His family felt that they had never liked him so much before. It seemed almost as if there were some truth in the theory of the Moderate Murderer.

On the other hand, Sir Harry Smythe, usually so much more good-humoured with his family, seemed to be in an increasingly bad humour. The dark red of his complexion deepened, until by contrast there was something almost alarming about the light of his pale eyes.

'I tell you of all these measly, meddlesome blighters,' he began.

'And I tell you you know nothing about it,' retorted his sister-in-law. 'He isn't a bit like that; he – '

At this point, for some reason or other, it was Olive who intervened swiftly and quietly; she looked a little wan and worried.

'Don't let's talk about all that now,' she said hastily. 'Harry has got such a lot of things to do. . . .'

'I know what I'm going to do,' said Barbara stubbornly. 'I'm going to ask Lord Tallboys, as Governor of this place, if he will let me visit Mr. Hume and see if I can find out what it means.'

She had become for some reason violently excited and her own voice sounded strangely in her ears. She had a dizzy impression of Harry Smythe's eyes standing out of his head in apoplectic anger and of Olive's face in the background growing more and more unnaturally pale and staring; and hovering over all, with something approaching to an elvish mockery, the benevolent amusement of her uncle. She felt as if he had let out too much, or that he had gained a new subtlety of perception.

Meanwhile John Hume was sitting in his place of detention, staring at a blank wall with an equally blank face. Accustomed as he was to solitude, he soon found something of a strain in two or three days and nights of the dehumanised solitude of imprisonment. Perhaps the fact most vivid to his immediate senses was being deprived of tobacco. But he had other and what some would call graver grounds of depression. He did not know what sort of sentence he would be likely to get for confessing to an attempt to wound the Governor. But he knew enough of political conditions and legal expedients to know that it would be easy to inflict heavy punishment immediately after the public scandal of the crime. He had lived in that outpost of civilization for the last ten years, till Tallboys had picked him up in Cairo; he remembered the violent reaction after the murder of the previous Governor, the way in which the Deputy-Governor had been able to turn himself into a despot and sweep the country with coercion acts and punitive expeditions, until his impulsive militarism had been a little moderated by the arrival of Tallboys with a compromise from the home Government. Tallboys was still alive and even, in a modified manner, kicking. But he was probably still under doctor's orders and could hardly be judge in his own cause; so that the autocratic Smythe would probably have another chance of riding the whirlwind and directing the storm. But the truth is that there was at the back of the prisoner's mind something that he feared much more than prison. The tiny point of panic, which had begun to worry and eat away even his rocky stolidity of mind and body, was the fear that his fantastic explanation had given his enemies another sort of opportunity. What he really feared was their saying he was mad and putting him under more humane and hygienic treatment.

And indeed, anyone watching his demeanour for the next hour or so might be excused for entertaining doubts and fancies on the point. He was still staring before him in a rather strange fashion. But he was no longer staring as if he saw nothing; but rather as if he saw something. It seemed to himself that, like a hermit in his cell, he was seeing visions.

'Well, I suppose I am, after all,' he said aloud in a dead and distinct voice. 'Didn't St. Paul say something? . . . Wherefore, O King Agrippa, I was not disobedient to the heavenly vision. . . . I have seen that heavenly one coming in at the door like that several times; and rather hoped it was real. But real people can't come through prison doors like that. . . . Once it came so that the room might have been full of trumpets and once with a cry like the wind and there was a fight and I found out that I could hate and that I could love. Two miracles on one night. Don't you think that must have been a dream – that is supposing you weren't a dream and could think anything? But I did rather hope you were real then.'

'Don't!' said Barbara Traill, 'I am real now.'

'Do you mean to tell me in cold blood that I am not mad,' said Hume, still staring at her, 'and you are here?'

'You are the only sane person I ever knew,' she replied.

'Good Lord,' he said, 'then I've said a good deal just now

that ought only to be said in lunatic asylums – or in heavenly visions.'

'You have said so much,' she said in a low voice, 'that I want you to say much more. I mean about the whole of this trouble. After what you have said . . . don't you think I might be allowed to know?'

He frowned at the table and then said rather more abruptly:

'The trouble was that I thought you were the last person who ought to know. You see, there is your family; and you might be brought into it, and one might have to hold one's tongue for the sake of someone you would care about.'

'Well,' she said steadily, 'I *have* been brought into it for the sake of someone I care about.'

She paused a moment and went on: 'The others never did anything for me. They would have let me go raving mad in a respectable flat, and so long as I was finished at a fashionable school, they wouldn't have cared if I'd finished myself with laudanum. I never really talked to anybody before. I don't want to talk to anybody else now.'

He sprang to his feet; something like an earthquake had shaken him at last out of his long petrified incredulity about happiness. He caught her by both hands and words came out of him he had never dreamed were within. And she, who was younger in years, only stared at him with a steady smile and starry eyes, as if she were older and wiser; and at the end only said:

'You will tell me now.'

'You must understand,' he said at last more soberly, 'that what I said was true. I was not making up fairy-tales to shield my long-lost brother from Australia, or any of that business in the novels. I really did put that bullet in your uncle, and I meant to put it there.'

'I know,' she said, 'but for all that I'm sure I don't know everything. I'm sure there is some extraordinary story behind all this.'

'No,' he answered. 'It isn't an extraordinary story; except an extraordinarily ordinary story.'

He paused a moment reflectively and then went on:

'It's really a particularly plain and simple story. I wonder it hasn't happened hundreds of times before. I wonder it hasn't been told in hundreds of stories before. It might so easily happen anywhere, given certain conditions.

'In this case you know some of the conditions. You know that sort of balcony that runs round my bungalow; and how one looks down from it and sees the whole landscape like a map. Well, I was looking down and saw all that flat plan of the place; the row of villas and the wall and path running behind it and the sycamore, and further on the olives and the end of the wall, and so out into the open slopes being laid out with turf and all the rest. But I saw what surprised me; that the rifle-range was already set up. It must have been a rush order; people must have worked all night. And even as I stared I saw in the distance a dot that was a man standing by the nearest target, as if adding the last touches. Then he made a sort of signal to somebody away on there other side and moved very rapidly away from the place. Tiny as the figure looked, every gesture told me something; he was quite obviously clearing out just before the firing at the target was to begin. And almost at the same moment I saw something else. Well, I saw one thing, anyhow. I saw why Lady Smythe is worried and wandered distracted in the garden.'

Barbara stared; but he went on: 'Travelling along the path from the Governorate and towards the sycamore was a familiar shape. It just showed above the long garden wall in sharp outline like a shape in a shadow pantomime. It was the top-hat of Lord Tallboys. Then I remembered that he always went for a constitutional along this path and out on to the slopes beyond; and I felt an overwhelming suspicion that he did not know that the space beyond was already a firing-ground. You know he is very deaf; and I sometimes doubt whether he hears all the things officially told to him; sometimes I fear they are told so that he cannot hear. Anyhow, he had every appearance of marching straight across as usual; and there came over me in a cataract a solid, an overwhelming and a most shocking certainty.

'I will not say much about that now. I will say as little as I can for the rest of my life. But there were things I knew and you probably don't about the politics here and what had led up to that dreadful moment. Enough that I had good reason for my dread. Feeling vaguely that if things were interrupted there might be a fight, I snatched up my own gun and dashed down the slope towards the path, waving wildly and trying to hail or head him off. He didn't see me and couldn't hear me. I pounded along after him along the path, but he had too long a start. By the time I reached the sycamore, I knew I was too late. He was already half-way down the grove of olives and no mortal runner could reach him before he came to the corner.

'I felt a rage against the fool which a man looks against the background of fate. I saw his lean pompous figure with the absurd top-hat riding on top of it; and the large ears standing out from his head . . . the large, useless ears. There was something agonizingly grotesque about that unconscious back outlined against the plains of death. For I was certain that the moment he passed the corner that field would be swept by the fire, which would cut across at right angles to his progress. I could think of only one thing to do and I did it. Hayter thought I was mad when I asked him if he had ever hanged a man to prevent his being hanged. That is the sort of practical joke I played. I shot a man to prevent his being shot.

'I put a bullet in his calf and he dropped, about two yards from the corner. I waited a moment and saw that people were coming out of the last houses to pick him up. I did the only thing I really regret. I had a vague idea the house by the sycamore was empty, so I threw the gun over the wall into the garden, and nearly got that poor old ass of a parson into trouble. Then I went home and waited till they summoned me to give evidence about Gregory.'

He concluded with all his normal composure, but the girl was still staring at him with an abnormal attention and even alarm.

'But what was it all about,' she asked; 'who could have –?'

'It was one of the best planned things I ever knew,' he said.

'I don't believe I could have proved anything. It would have looked just like an accident.'

'You mean,' she said, 'that it wouldn't have been.'

'As I said before, I don't want to say much about that now, but . . . Look here, you are the sort of person who likes to think about things. I'll just ask you to take two things and think about them; and then you can get used to the idea in your own way.

'The first thing is this. I am a Moderate, as I told you; I really am against all the Extremists. But when journalists and jolly fellows in clubs say that, they generally forget that there really are different sorts of Extremists. In practice they think only of revolutionary Extremists. Believe me, the reactionary Extremists are quite as likely to go to extremes. The history of faction fights will show acts of violence by Patricians as well as Plebeians, by Ghibellines as well as Guelphs, by Orangemen as well as Fenians, by Facists as well as Bolshevists, by the Ku-Klux-Klan as well as the Black Hand. And when a politician comes from London with a compromise in his pocket – it is not only Nationalists who see their plans frustrated.

'The other point is more personal, especially to you. You once told me you feared for the family sanity, merely because you had bad dreams and brooded over things of your own imagination. Believe me, it's not the imaginative people who become insane. It's not they who are mad, even when they are morbid. They can always be woken up from bad dreams by broader prospects and brighter visions – because they are imaginative. The stubborn stoical men who have only room for one idea and take it literally. The sort of man who seems to be silent but stuffed to bursting, congested –'

'I know,' she said hastily; 'you needn't say it, because I believe I understand everything now. Let me tell you two things also; they are shorter; but they have to do with it. My uncle sent me here with an officer who has an order for your release . . . and the Deputy-Governor is going home . . . resignation on the grounds of ill-health.'

'Tallboys is no fool,' said John Hume, 'he has guessed.'

She laughed with a little air of embarrassment.

'I'm afraid he has guessed a good many things.' she said.

What the other things were is no necessary part of this story; but Hume proceeded to talk about them at considerable length during the rest of the interview; until the lady herself was moved to a somewhat belated protest. She said she did not believe that he could really be a Moderate after all.

5
THE TOWER OF TREASON

At a certain moment, just before sunset, a young man was walking in a rather extraordinary fashion across a wild country bearded with grey and wintry forests. In the solitude of that silent and wooded wilderness he was walking backwards. There was nobody to notice the eccentricity; it could not arrest the rush of the eagles over those endless forests where Hungarian frontiers fade into the Balkans; it could not be expected to arouse criticism in the squirrel or the hare. Even the peasants of those parts might possibly have been content to explain it as the vow of a pilgrim, or some other wild religious exercise; for it was a land of wild religious exercises. Only a little way in front of him (or rather, at that instant behind him), the goal of his journey and many previous journeys, was a strange half-military monastery, like some old chapel of the Templars, where vigilant ascetics watched night and day over a hoard of sacred jewels, guarded at once like the crown of a king and the relic of a saint. Barely a league beyond, where the hills began to lift themselves clear of the forest, was a yet more solitary outpost of such devotional seclusion; a hermitage which held captive a man once famous through half Europe, a dazzling diplomatist and ambitious statesman, now solitary and only rarely visited by the religious, for whom he was supposed to have more invisible jewels of a new wisdom. All that land, that seemed so silent and empty, was alive with such miracles.

Nevertheless the young man was not performing a religious vow, or going on a religious pilgrimage. He had himself known personally the renowned recluse of the hermitage on the hill, when they were both equally in the world and worldly; but he had not the faintest intention of following his holy example. He was himself a guest of the monastery that was the consecrated casket of the strange jewels; but his errand was purely political and not in the least consecrated. He was a diplomatist by profession; but it must not be lightly inferred that he was walking backwards out of excessive deference to the etiquette of courts. He was an Englishman by nationality; but he was not, with somewhat distant reverence, still walking backwards before the King of England. Nor was he paying so polite a duty to any other king, though he might himself have said that he was paying it to a queen. In short the explanation of his antic, as of not a few antics, was that he was in love; a condition common in romances and not unknown in real life. He was looking backwards at the house he had just left, in an abstracted or distracted fashion, half hoping to see a last signal from it or merely to catch a last glimpse of it among the trees. And his look was the more longing and lingering on this particular evening, for an atmospheric reason he would have found it hard to explain: a sense of pathos and distance and division hardly explained by his practical difficulties. As the sunset clouds were heavy with a purple which typifies the rich tragedy of Lent, so on this evening passion seemed to weigh on him with something of the power of doom. And a pagan of the mystical sort would certainly have called what happened next an omen; though a practical man of the modern sort might rather have hinted that it was the highly calculable effect of walking backwards and being a fool. A noise of distant firing was heard in the forest; and the slight start he gave, combined with a loop of grass that caught his foot, threw him sprawling all his length; as if that distant shot had brought him down.

But the omens were not all ended; nor could they all be counted pagan. For as he gazed upwards for an instant, from the place where he had fallen, he saw above the black forest and against the vivid violet clouds, something strangely suitable to that tragic purple recalling the traditions of Lent. It was a great face between out-stretched gigantic arms; the face upon a large wooden crucifix. The figure was carved in the round but very much in the rough, in a rude archaic style, and was probably an old outpost of Latin Christianity in that labyrinth of religious frontiers. He must have seen it before, for it stood on a little hill in a clearing of the woods, just opposite the one straight path leading to the sanctuary of the jewels, the tower of which could already be seen rising out of the sea of leaves. But somehow the size of the head above the trees, seen suddenly from below after the shock of the fall, had the look of a judgment in the sky. It seemed a strange fate to have fallen at the foot of it.

The young man, whose name was Bertram Drake, came from Cambridge and was heir to all the comforts and conventions of scepticism, further enlivened by a certain impatience in his own intellectual temper, which made him more mutinous than was good for his professional career; an active, restless man with a dark but open audacious face. But for an instant something had stirred in him which is Christendom buried in Europe; something which is a memory even where it is a myth. Rising, he turned a troubled gaze to the great circle of dark grey forests, out of which rose in the distance the lonely tower of his destination; and even as he did so he saw something else. A few feet from where he had just fallen, and risen again to his feet, lay another fallen figure. And the figure did not rise.

He strode across, bent down over the body and touched it, and was soon grimly satisfied about why it was lying still. Nor was it without a further shock; for he even realized that he had seen the man before, though in a sufficiently casual and commonplace fashion; as a rustic bringing timber to the house he had just left. He recognized the spectacles on the square and stolid face; they were horn spectacles of the plainest pattern, yet they did not somehow suit his figure, which was clothed loosely like an ordinary peasant. And in the tragedy of the moment they were almost grotesque. The very fixity of the spectacles on the face was one of those details of daily habit that suddenly made death incredible. He had looked down at him for several seconds, before he became conscious that the deathly silence around was in truth a living silence; he was not alone.

A yard or two away an armed man was standing like a statue. He was a stalwart but rather stooping figure, with a long antiquated musket slung aslant on his shoulders; and in his hand a drawn sabre shone like a silver crescent. For the rest, he was a long-coated, long-bearded figure with a faint suggestion, to be felt in some figures from Russia and Eastern Europe generally, that the coats were like skirts and that the big beard has some of the terrors of a hairy mask; a faint touch of the true East. Thus accoutered, it had the look of a rude uniform; but the Englishman knew it was not that of the small Slav state in which he stood; which may be called, for the purpose of this tale, the kingdom of Transylvania. But when Drake addressed him in the language of that country, with which he himself was already fairly familiar, it was clear enough that the stranger understood. And there was a final touch of something strange in the fact that the brown eyes of this bearded barbaric figure seemed not only sad but even soft, as with a sort of mystification of their own.

'Have you murdered this man?' asked the Englishman sternly.

The other shook his head; and then answered an incredulous stare by the simple but sufficient gesture of holding out his bare sabre immediately under the inquirer's eyes. It was an unanswerable fact that the blade was quite clean and without a spot of blood.

'But you were going to murder him,' aid Drake. 'Why did you draw your sword?'

'I was going to -' and with that the stranger stopped in his speech, hesitated, and then suddenly slapping his sabre back into the sheath, dived into the bushes and disappeared, before Drake could make a movement in pursuit of him.

The echoes of the original volley that had waked the woods had not long died away on the distant heights beyond the tower; and Drake could now only suppose that the shot thus fired had been the real cause of death. He was convinced, for many causes, that the shot had come from the tower; and he had other reasons for rapidly repairing thither besides the necessity of giving the fatal news to the nearest habitation. He hurried along the very straight and strictly embanked road that was like a bridge between the tower and the little hill in front of the crucifix; and soon came under the shadow of the strange monastic building, now enormous in scale though simple in outline. For though it was as wide in its circle as a great camp, and even bore on its flat top a sort of roof garden large enough to allow a little exercise to its permanent guards and captives, it rose sheer from the ground in a single round and windowless wall; so high that it stood up in the landscape almost like a pillar rather than a tower. The straight road to it ended in one narrow bridge across a deep but dry moat, outside which ran a ring of thorny hedges, but inside which rose great grisly iron spikes; giant thorns such as are made by man. The completeness of its enclosure and isolation was part of an ancient national policy for the protection of an ancient national prize. For the building and the men in it were devoted to the defence of the treasure known as the Coat of the Hundred Stones, though there were now rather less than that number to be defended. According to the legend, the great King Hector, the almost prehistoric hero of those hills, had a corslet or breastplate which was a cluster of countless small diamonds, as a substitute for chain mail; and in old dim pictures and tapestries he was always shown riding into battle as if in a vesture of stars. The legend had ramifications in neighbouring and rival realms; and therefore the possession of this relic was a point of national and international importance in that land of legends. The legend may have been false; but the little loose jewels or what were left of them, were real enough.

Drake stood looking at that sombre stronghold in an equally sombre spirit. It was the end of winter, and the grey woods were already just faintly empurpled with that suppressed and nameless bloom which is a foreshadowing rather than a beginning of the spring, but his own mood at the moment, though romantic, was also tragic. The string of strange events he had left in his track, if they had not arrested him as omens, must still have arrested him as enigmas. The man killed for no reason, the sword drawn for no reason, the speech broken short also for no reason, all these incidents affected him like the images in a warning dream. He felt that a cloud was on his destiny; nor was he wrong, so far at least as that evening's journey carried him. For when he re-entered that militant monastery of which he was the guest, a new catastrophe befell him. And when next day he retraced his steps on the woodland path along which he had been looking when he fell, and when he came again to the house towards which he had looked so longingly, he found its door shut against him.

On the day following he was striding desperately along a new path, winding upwards through the woods to the hills beyond, with his back both to the house and the tower. For something, as has been hinted, had befallen him in the last few days which was not only a tragedy but a riddle; and it was only when he reviewed the whole in the light, or darkness, of his last disaster, that he remembered that he had one old friend in that land, and one who was a reader of such riddles. He was making his way to the hermitage that was the home – some might almost say the grave – of a great man now known only as Father Stephen, though his real name had once been scrawled on the historic treaties and sprawled in the newspaper headlines of many nations. There is no space here to tell all the activities of his once famous acumen. In the world of what has come to be called secret diplomacy he was something more than a secret diplomatist. He was one from whom no diplomacy could be kept secret. Something of his later mysticism, and appreciation of moods and of the subconscious mind, had even helped him; he not only saw small things, but he saw them as large things, and largely. It was he who had anticipated the suicide of a cosmopolitan millionaire judging from an atmosphere and the fact that he did not wind up his watch. It was he also who had frustrated a great German conspiracy in America, detecting the Teutonic spy by his unembarrassed posture in a chair when a Boston lady was handing him tea. Now, at long and rare intervals, he would become conscious of such external problems; and, in cases of great injustice, use the same powers to track a lost sheep, or recover the little hoard stolen from the stocking of a peasant.

A long terrace of low cliffs or rocks hollowed here and there ran along the top of a desolate slope that swept down and vanished amid the highest horns and crests of the winter trees.

When this wall faced the rising of the sun, the stone shone pale like marble; and in one place especially had the squared look of a human building, pierced by an unquestionably human entrance. In the white wall was a black doorway, hollow and almost horrible like a ghost; for it was shaped in the rude outline of a man, with head and shoulders, like a mummy-case. There was no other mark about this coffin-like cavity, except just beside it a flat coloured icon of the Holy Family, drawn in that extreme decorative style of Eastern Christianity, which make a gaily painted diagram rather than a picture. But its gold and scarlet and green and sky-blue glittered on the rock by the black hole like some fabled butterfly from the mouth of the grave. But Bertram Drake strode to the gate of that grave and called aloud, as if upon the name of the dead.

To put the truth in a paradox, he had expected the resurrection to surprise him, and yet he was surprised unexpectedly. When he had last met his famous friend, in evening dress in the stalls of a great theatre in Vienna, he had found that friend pale and prematurely old, and his wit dreary and cynical. He even vaguely remembered the matter of their momentary conversation, some disenchanted criticism about the drop-scene or curtain, in which the great diplomatist had seemed a shade more interested than in the play. But when the same man came out of that black hole in the bleak mountains he seemed to have recovered an almost unnatural youth and even childhood. The colours had come back into his strong face; and his eyes shone as he came out of the shadow, almost as an animal's will shine in the dark. The tonsure had left him a ring of chestnut hair, and his tall bony figure seemed less loose and more erect than of old. All this might be very rationally explained by the strong air and simple life of the hills; but his visitor pursued and tormented by fancies, felt for the moment as if the man had a secret sun or fountain of life in that black chamber, or drew nourishment from the roots of the mountains.

He commented on the change in the first few greetings that passed between them; and the hermit seemed willing, though hardly able, to describe the nature of his acceptance of his strange estate.

'This is the last I shall see of this earth,' he said quietly, 'and I am more than contented in letting it pass. Yet I do not value it less, but rather I think more, as it simplifies itself to a single hold on life. What I know, with assurance, is that it is well for me to remain here, and to stray nowhere else.'

After a silence he added, gazing with his burning blue eyes across the wooded valley: 'Do you remember when we last met at that theatre and I told you that I always liked the picture on the curtain as much as the scenes of the play. It was some village landscape, I remember, with a bridge, and I felt perversely that I should like to lean on the bridge or look into the little houses. And then I remembered that from almost any other angle I should see it was only a thin painted rag. That is how I feel about this world, as I see it from this mountain. Not that it is not beautiful, for after all a curtain can be beautiful. Not even that it is unreal, for after all a curtain is real. But only that it is thin, and that the things behind it are the real drama. And I feel that when I shift my place, it will be the end. I shall hear the three thuds of the mallet in the French theatres; and the curtain will rise. I shall be dead.'

The Englishman made an effort to shake off the clouds of mystery that had always been so uncongenial to him. 'Frankly,' he said, 'I can't profess to understand how a man of your intellect can brood in that superstitious way. You look healthy enough, but your mind is surely the more morbid for it. Do you really mean to tell me it would be a sin to leave this rat-hole?'

'No,' answered the other, 'I do not say it would be sin. I only say it would be death. It might conceivably be my duty to go down into the world again; in that case it would be my duty to die. It would have been my duty at any time when I was a soldier; but I never should have done it so cheerfully. Now, if ever I see my signal in the distance, I shall rise and leave this cavern, and leave this world.'

'How can you possibly tell?' cried Drake in his impatient way. 'Living alone in this wilderness you think you know everything, like a lunatic. Does nobody ever come to see you?'

'Oh, yes,' replied Father Stephen with a smile. 'The people from round here sometimes come up and ask me questions; they seem to have a notion that I can help them out of their difficulties.'

The dark vivacity of Drake's face took on a shade of something like shame, as he laughed uneasily and answered.

'And I ought to apologise for what I said just now about the lunatic. For I've come up here on the same errand myself. The truth is I have a notion that you can help me out of *my* difficulties.'

'I will do my best,' replied Father Stephen. 'I am afraid they have troubled you a good deal, by the look of you.'

They sat down side by side on a flat rock near the edge of the slope, and Bertram Drake began to tell the whole of his story, or all of it that he needed to tell.

'I needn't tell you,' he began, 'why I am in this country, or why I have been so long a guest in that place where they keep the Coat of the Hundred Stones. You know better than anybody, for it was you who originally wanted an English representative here to write a report on their preservation, for the old propaganda purpose we know of. You probably also knew that the rules of that strange institution put even a friendly, and I may say an honoured guest under very severe restrictions. They are so horribly afraid of any traffic with the outside world that I have had to be practically a prisoner. But the arrangements are stricter even than they were in your visiting days; ever since Paul the new Abbot came from across the hills. I don't think you've seen him; nobody's seen him outside the monastery; and I couldn't describe him any more than I could describe you. But while you, somehow, still seem to include all kind of things, like the circle of the world, he seems to be only one thing, like the point that is the pivot of a circle. He is as still as the centre of a whirlpool. I mean there seems to be direction and a driving speed in his very immobility; but all pointed and simplified to a single thing: the guarding of the diamonds. He has repaired and made rigid the scheme of defence till I really do not think that loss or leakage from that treasure would be physically possible. Suffice it to say for the moment that it is kept in a casket of steel, in the centre of the roof garden, watched by the brethren who sleep only in rotation, and especially by the old abbot himself who hardly sleeps at all, except for a few hours just before and after sunset. And even then he sleeps sitting beside the casket, with which no man may meddle but himself, and with his hand on his heavy old gun, an antiquated blunderbuss enough, but with which he can shoot very straight for all that. Then sometimes he will wake quite softly and suddenly; and sit looking up that straight road to where the crucifix stands, like a hoary old white eagle. His watch is his world; though in every other way he is mild and benevolent, though he gave orders for the feeding of the poor for miles around, yet if he hears a footstep or faint movement anywhere in the woods around, except on the road that is the recognized approach, he will shoot without mercy as at a wolf. I have reason to know this, as you shall hear.

'Anyhow, as I said, you know that the rules were always strict, and now they're stricter than ever. I was only able to enter the place by being hoisted up by a sort of crane or open-air lift, which it takes several of the monks together to work from the top; and I wasn't supposed to leave the place at all. It is possible that you also know, for you read people so rapidly like pictures rather than books, that I am a most unfortunate sort of brute to be chained by the leg in that way. My faults are all impatience and irreverence; and you may guess that, in a week or two, I might have felt inclined to burn the place down. But you cannot know the real and special reason that made my slavery intolerable.'

'I am sorry,' said Father Stephen; and the sincerity of the note again brought Drake's impatience to a standstill with abrupt self-reproach.

'Heaven knows it is I who should be sorry; I have been greatly to blame,' he said. 'But even if you call what I did a sin, you will see that it had a punishment. In one word, you are speaking to a man to whom no one this country will speak. A monstrous accusation rests upon me, which I cannot refute, and have only some faint hope that you may refute for me. Hundreds in that valley below us are probably cursing my name, and even crying out for my death. And yet, I think, of all those scores of souls looking at me with suspicion, there is only one from whom I cannot endure it.'

'Does he live near here?' inquired the hermit.

'She does,' replied the Englishman.

An irony shining in the eyes of the anchorite suggested that the answer was not quite unexpected; but he said nothing till the other resumed his tale.

'You know that sort of château that some French nobleman, an exiled prince I believe, built upon the wooded ridge over there beyond the crucifix – you can just see its turrets from here. I'm not sure who owns it now; but it's been rented for some years now by Dr. Amiel, a famous physician, a Frenchman, or, rather, a French Jew. He is supposed to have high humanitarian ideals, including the idealization of this small nationality here, which, of course, suits our Foreign Office very well. Perhaps it's unfair to say he's only 'supposed' to be this; and the plain truth is I'm not a fair judge of the man, for a reason you may soon guess. But apart from sentiment, I think somehow I am in two minds about him. It sounds absurd to say that like or dislike of a man could depend on his wearing a red smoking-cap. But that's the nearest I can get to it; bare-headed and just a little bald-headed, he seems only a dark, rather distinguished-looking French man of science, with a pointed beard. When he puts that red fez on he is suddenly something much lower than a Turk; and I see all Asia sneering and leering at me across the Levant. Well, perhaps it's a fancy of the fit I'm in; and it's only just to say that people believe in him, who are really devoted to this people or to our policy here. The people staying with him now, and during the few weeks I was there, are English and very keen on the cause, and they say his work has been splendid. A young fellow named Woodville, from my own college, who has travelled a lot, and written some books about yachting, I think. And his sister.'

'Your story is very clear so far,' observed Father Stephen with restraint.

Drake seemed suddenly moved to impetuosity. 'I know I'm in a mad state and had no right to call you morbid; and it's a state in which it's awfully difficult to judge of people. How is it that two people, just a brother and sister, can be so alike and so different? They're both what is called good-looking; and even good-looking in the same way. Why on earth should her high colour look as clear as if it were pale, while his offends me as if it were painted? Why should I think of her hair as gold and look at his as if it were gilt? Honestly, I can't help feeling something artificial about him; but I didn't come to trouble you with these prejudices. There is little or nothing to be said against Woodville; he has something of a name for betting on horses, but not enough to disturb any man of the world. I think the reputation has rather dogged his footsteps in the shape of his servant, Grimes, who is much more horsy than his master, and much in evidence. You see there were few servants at the château, even the gardening being done by a peasant from outside; an unfortunate fellow in horn spectacles who come into this story later. Anyhow, Woodville was, or professed to be, quite sound in his politics about this place; and I really think him sincere about it. And as for his sister, she has an enthusiasm that is as beautiful as Joan of Arc.'

There was a short silence, and then Father Stephen said dreamily: 'In short, you somehow escaped from your prison, and paid her a visit.'

'Three visits,' relied Drake, with an embarrassed laugh. 'and nearly broke my neck at the end of a rope, besides being repeatedly shot at with a gun. I'll tell you later on, if you want them, all the details of how I managed to slip out and in again during those sunset hours of Abbot Paul's slumbers. They really resolved themselves into two; the accidental discovery of a disused iron chain, that had been used for the crane or lift, and the character of the old monk who happened to be watching while the Abbot slept. How indescribable is a man, and how huge are the things that turn on his unique self as on a hinge!

All those monks were utterly incorruptible, and I owed it to a sympathy that was almost mockery. In an English romance, I suppose, my confederate would have been a young mutinous monk, dreaming of the loves he had lost; whereas my friend was one of the oldest, utterly loyal to the religious life, and helping me from a sort of whim that was little more than a lark. Can you imagine a sort of innocent Pandarus, or even a Christian Pan! He would have died rather than betray the holy stones; but when he was convinced that my love affair was honourable in itself, he let me down by the chain in fits of silent laughter, like a grinning old goblin. It was a pretty wild experience, I can tell you, swinging on that loose iron ladder, like dropping off the earth on a falling star. But I swung myself somehow clear of the spikes below, and crept along under the thick wood by the side of the road. Even as I did so came the crack and rolling echoes of the musket on the tower; and a tuft, from a fir tree spreading above me, dropped detached upon the road at my right. A terrible old man, the Abbot. A light sleeper.'

Both men were gazing at the strange tower that rose out of the distant woods as Drake, after a pause, renewed his narrative.

'There is a high hedge of juniper and laurel at the bottom of the garden of Dr. Amiel's château. At least it is high on the outer side, rising above a sort of ledge of earth on the slope, but comparatively low when seen from the level garden above. I used to climb up to this ledge in that late afternoon twilight, and she used to come down the garden, with the lights of the house almost clinging about her dress, and we used to talk. It's no good talking to you about what she looked like, with her hair all as yellow light behind the leaves; though those are the sort of things that make my present position a hell. You are a monk and not – I fear I was going to say not a man; but at any rate not a lover.'

'I am not a juniper bush, if the argument be conclusive.' remarked Father Stephen. 'But I can admire it in its place; and I know that many good things grow wild in the garden of God. But, if I may say so, seeing that so honourable a lady received such rather eccentric attentions from you, I cannot see that you have much reason to be jealous of the poor Jewish gentleman, as you seem to be, even if he is so base and perfidious as to wear a smoking-cap.'

'What you say was true until yesterday,' said Drake. 'I know now that until yesterday I was in paradise. But I had gone there once too often; and on my third return journey a thunderbolt struck me down, worse than any bullet from the tower. The old Abbot had never discovered my own evasion; but he must have had miraculous hearing when he woke, for every time I crept through the thicket, as softly as I could, he must have heard something moving, and fired again and again. Well, the last time I found the spectacled peasant who worked for Dr. Amiel, he was lying dead, a little way in front of the cross, and a foreign-looking fellow with a drawn sabre standing near him. But the strange thing was that the sabre was unstained and unused, and I was eventually convinced that one of the Abbot's shot must have killed the poor peasant in the goggles. Revolving all these things in growing doubt, I returned to the tower, and saw an ominous thing. The regular mechanical lift was lowered for me; and when I re-entered the place, I found that all my escapade had been discovered. But I found something far worse.

'When all those faces were turned upon me, faces I shall never forget, I knew I was being judged for something more that a love-affair. My poor old friend, who had connived at my escape, would not have been so much prostrated for the lesser matter; and as for the Abbot, the form of his countenance was changed, as it says in the Bible, by something nearer to his own lonely soul than all such lesser matters. Well, the truth of this tragedy is soon told. For the last week, as it appeared, the hoard of the little diamonds had dwindled, no man could imagine how. They were counted by the Abbot and two monks at certain regular intervals; and it was found that the losses had occurred at definite intervals also. Finally, there was found another fact; a fact of which I can make no sense; yet a fact to which I can find no answer. After each of my secret visits to the château, and then only, some of the diamonds had disappeared.

'I have not even the right to ask you to believe in my

innocence. No man alive in the whole great landscape we are looking at believes in my innocence. I do not know what would have happened to me, or whether I should have been killed by the monks or the peasants, if I had not appealed to your great authority in this country; and if the Abbot had not been persuaded at last to allow the appeal. Dr. Amiel thinks I am guilty. Woodville thinks I am guilty. His sister I have not even been able to see.'

There was another silence, and then Father Stephen remarked rather absently:

'Does he wear slippers as well as a smoking-cap?'

'Do you mean the doctor? No. What on earth do you mean?'

'Nothing at all, if he doesn't. There's no more to be said about that. Well, it's pretty obvious, I suppose, what are the next three questions. First, I suppose the woodman carried an axe. Did he ever carry a pickaxe? Did he ever carry any other tool in particular? Second, did you ever happen to hear anything like a bell? About the time you heard the shot, for instance? But that will probably have occurred to you already. And third, amid such plain preliminaries in the matter, is Dr. Amiel fond of birds?'

There was again a shadow of irony in the simplicity of the recluse; and Drake turned his dark face towards him with a doubtful frown.

'Are you making fun of me?' he asked. 'I should prefer to know.'

'I believe in your innocence, if that is what you mean,' replied Father Stephen, 'and, believe me, I am beginning at the right end in order to establish it.'

'But who could it be?' cried Drake in his rather irritable fashion. 'I'll tell the plain truth, even against myself, and I'd swear all those monks were really startled out of their wits. And even the peasants near here, supposing they could get into the tower, which they can't – why I'd be as much surprised to hear of them desecrating the Hundred Stones as if I heard they'd all suddenly become Plymouth Brethren this morning. No; suspicion is sure to fall on the foreigners, like myself; and none of the others round here have a case against them, as I have. Woodville may have a few racing debts; but I'd never believe this about *her* brother, little as I happened to like him. And as for Dr. Amiel – ' And he stopped, his face darkening with thought.

'Yes, but that's beginning at the wrong end,' observed Father Stephen, 'because it's beginning with all the millions of mankind, and every man a mystery. I am trying to find out who stole the stones; you seem to be trying to find out who wanted to steal them. Believe me, the smaller and more practical question is also the larger and more philosophical. To the shades of possible wanting there is hardly any limit. It is the root of all religion that anybody may be almost anything if he chooses. The cynics are wrong, not because they say that heroes may be cowards, but because they do not see that the cowards may be heroes. Now you may think my remark about keeping birds very wild and your remark about betting on horses very relevant, but I assure you it is the other way around; for yours dealt with what might be thought, but mine with what could be done. Do you remember that German Prime Minister who was assassinated because he had reduced Russia to starvation? Millions of peasants might have wanted to murder him; but how could a moujik in Muscovy murder him in a theatre in Munich? He was murdered by a man who came there because he was a trained Russian dancer, and escaped from there because he was a trained Russian acrobat. That is, the highly offensive statesman in question was not killed by all the Russians who may have wanted to kill him; but the one Russian who *could* kill him. Well, you are the only approximate acrobat in this performance, and, apart from what I know about you I don't see how you could have burgled a safe inside the tower merely by dangling at the end of a string outside it. For the real enigma and obstacle in this story is not the stone tower, but the steel casket. I do not see how *you* could have stolen the jewels. I don't see how *anybody* could have stolen them. That is the hopeful part of it.'

'You are pretty paradoxical to-day,' growled his English friend.

'I am quite practical,' answered Stephen serenely. 'That is the starting-point, and it makes a good start. We have only to deal with a narrow number of conjectures about how it could just conceivably have been done. You scoffed at my three questions just now which I threw off when I was thinking rather about the preliminary approach to the tower. Well, I admit they were very long shots – indeed, very wild shots; I did not myself take them very seriously, or think they would lead to much. But they had this value: that they were not random guesses about the spiritual possibilities of everybody for a hundred miles round. They were the beginnings of an effort to bridge the real difficulties.'

'I am afraid,' observed Drake, 'that I did not realize that they were even that.'

'Well,' the hermit went on patiently, 'for the first problem of reaching the tower it was reasonable to think first, however hazily, of some sort of secret tunnel or subterranean entrance, and it was natural to ask if the strange workman at the château, who afterwards died so mysteriously, was seen carrying any excavating tools.'

'Well, I did think of that,' assented Drake, 'and I came to the conclusion that it was physically impossible. The inside of the tower is as plain and bare as a dry cistern and the floor is really solid concrete everywhere. But what did you mean by that second question about the bell?'

'What I confess still puzzles me,' said Father Stephen, 'even in your own story, is how the Abbot always heard a man threading his way through a thick forest so far below, so that he invariably fired after him, if only at a venture. Now, nothing would be more natural to such a scheme of defence than to set traps in the wood, in the way of burglar alarms, to warn the watchers in the tower. But anything like that would mean some system of wires or tubes passing through the wall into the woods, and anything of that sort I felt in a shadowy way, a very shadowy way indeed, might mean a passage for other things as well. It would destroy the argument of the sheer wall and the dead drop, which is at present an argument against you, since you alone dared to drop over it. And, of course, my third random question was of the same kind. Nothing could fly about the top of that high tower except birds. For I infer that the vigilant Paul was not too absent-minded to notice any large number of aeroplanes. Now, it is not in the least probable – it is, indeed, almost wildly improbable – but it is not *impossible*, that birds should be trained either to take messages or to commit thefts. Carrier pigeons do the former, and parrots and magpies have often done the latter. Dr. Amiel, being both a scientist and a humanitarian, I thought he might very well be a naturalist and an animal-lover. So if I had found his biological studies specializing wholly on the breeding of carrier pigeons, or if I had found all the love of his life lavished on a particular magpie, I should have thought the question worth following up, formidable as would have been the difficulties still threatening it as a solution.'

'I wish the love of his life *were* lavished on a magpie,' observed Bertram Drake bitterly. 'As it is, it's lavished on something else, and will be expected, I suppose, to flourish in the blight of mine. But, much as I hate him, I shouldn't like to say of him what he is probably saying of me.'

'There again is the mistaken method,' observed the other. 'probably he is not morally incapable of a really action; very few people are. That is why I stick to the point of whether he is materially capable. It would be quite easy to draw a dark suspicious picture both of him and Mr. Woodville. It is quite true that racing can be a raging gamble and that ruined gamblers are capable of almost anything. It is also true that nobody can be so much of a cad as a gentlemen when he is afraid of losing that title. In the same way, it is perfectly true that the Jews have woven over these nations a net that is not only international, but anti-national; and it is quite true that inhuman as is their usury and inhuman as is often their oppression of the poor, some of them are never so inhuman as when they are idealistic, never so inhuman as when they are humane. If we were talking about Amiel or about Woodville, instead of about you and about the diamonds, I could trace a thousand mystery stories in the matter. I could take your hint about the scarlet smoking-cap, and say it was a signal and the symbol of a secret society; that a hundred Jews in a hundred smoking-caps were plotting everywhere, as many of them really are; I could show you a conspiracy ramifying from the red cap of Amiel as it did from the *Bonnet Rouge* of Almereyda; or I could catch at your idle phrase about Woodville's hair looking gilded, and describe him as a monstrous decadent in a golden wig, a thing worthy of Nero. Very soon his horse-racing would have all the imperial insanity of charioteering in the amphitheatre, while his friend in the fez would be capable of carrying off Miss Woodville to a whole harem full of Miss Woodvilles, if you will pardon the image. But what corrects all this is the concrete difficulty I defined at the beginning. I still do not see how wearing either a red fez or a gilded wig could conjure very small gems out of a steel box at the top of a tower. But of course I did not mean to abandon all inquiry about the suspicious movements of anybody. I asked if the doctor wore slippers, on a remote chance in connexion with your steps having been heard in the wood, and I should like to know if you ever met anybody else prowling about in the forest.'

'Why, yes,' said Drake, with a slight start. 'I once met the man Grimes, now I remember it.'

'Mr. Woodville's servant,' remarked Father Stephen.

'Yes. A rat of a fellow with red hair,' Drake said, frowning. 'He seemed a bit startled to see me too.'

'Well, never mind,' answered the hermit. 'My own hair may well be called red, but I assure you I didn't steal the diamonds.'

'I never met anybody else,' went on Drake, 'except, of course, the mysterious man with the sabre and the dead man he was staring at. I think that is the queerest puzzle of all.'

'It is best to apply the same principle even to that,' replied his friend. 'It may be hard to imagine what a man could be doing with a drawn sword still unused. But, after all, there are a thousand things he might have been doing, from teaching the poor woodman to cut timber without an axe to cutting off the dead man's head for a trophy and a talisman, as some savages do. The question is whether felling the whole forest or filling the whole country with howling head-hunters would necessarily have got the stones out of the box.'

'He was certainly going to do something,' said Drake in a low voice. 'He said himself, 'I was going to,' and then he broke off and vanished. I was very profoundly persuaded, I hardly knew why, that there was something to be done to the dead man which could not be done till he was dead.'

'What?' asked the hermit, after an abrupt silence; and it sounded somehow like a new voice from a third person suddenly joining in the conversation.

'Which could not be done till he was dead,' repeated Drake, staring at him.

'Dead,' repeated Father Stephen.

And Drake, still staring at him, saw that his face, under its fringe of red hair, was as pale as his linen robe, and the eyes in it were blazing like the lost stones.

'So many things die,' he said. 'The birds I spoke about, flying and flashing about the great tower. Did you ever find a dead bird? Not one sparrow, it is written, falls to the ground without God. Even a dead bird would be precious. But a yet smaller thing will serve as a sign here.'

Drake, still gazing as his companion, felt a growing conviction that the man had suddenly gone mad. He said helplessly, 'What is the matter with you?' But Father Stephen had risen from his seat and was gazing calmly across the valley towards the west, which was all swimming with a golden sunlight that here and there turned the tops of the grey trees to silver.

'It is the thud of the mallet,' he said, 'and the curtain must rise.'

Something had certainly happened which the mind of Bertram Drake found it impossible at the moment to measure, but he remembered enough of the strange words with which their interview had opened to know that in some way the hermit was saying farewell to the hermitage and to many more human things. He asked some groping question, the very words of which he could not afterwards recall.

'I see my signal at last,' said Father Stephen. 'Treason stands up in my own land as that tower stands in the landscape. A great sin against the people and against the glory of the dead is raging in that valley like a lost battle. And I must go down and do my last office, as King Hector came down from these mountains to his last battle long ago, to that Battle of the Stones where he was slain and his sacred coat of mail so nearly captured. For the enemy has come again over the hills, though in a shape in which we never looked for him.'

The voice that had lingered with irony and shrewdness over the details of detection had the simplicity which makes poetry and primitive rhetoric still possible among such peoples. He was already marching down the slope, leaving Drake wavering in doubt, being uncertain to tell the truth, whether his own problem had not been rather lost in this last transition.

'Oh, do not fear for your own story,' said Father Stephen. 'The Battle of the Stones was a victory.'

As they went down the mountain-side Drake followed with a strange sense of travelling with some immobile thing liberated by a miracle, as if the earth were shaken by a stone statue walking. The statue led him a strange and rather erratic dance, however, covering considerable time and distance, and the great cloud in the west was a sunset cloud before they came to their final halt. Rather to Drake's surprise, they passed the tower of the monastery, and already seemed to be passing under the shadow of the great wooden cross in the woods.

'We shall return this way to-night.' said Stephen, speaking for the first time on their march. 'The sin upon this land to-night lies so heavy that there is no other way. *Via Crucis*.'

'Why do you talk in this terrible way?' broke out Drake abruptly. 'Don't you realize that it's enough to make a man like me hate the cross? Indeed, I think by this time I really do. Remember what my story is, and what once made these woodlands wonderful to me. Would you blame me if the god I saw among the trees was a pagan god, and at any rate a happy one? This is a wild garden that was full, for me, of love and laughter; and I look up and see that image blackening the sun and saying that the world is utterly evil.'

'You do not understand,' replied Father Stephen quite quietly. 'If there are any who stand apart merely because the world is utterly evil, they are not old monks like me; they are much more likely to be young Byronic disappointed lovers like you. No, it is the optimist much more than the pessimist who finally finds the cross waiting for him at the end of his own road. It is the thing that remains when all is said, like the payment after the feast. Christendom is full of feasts, but they bear the names of martyrs who won them in torments. And if such things horrify you, go and ask what torments your English soldiers endure for the land which your English poets praise. Go and see your English children playing with fireworks, and you will find one of their toys is named after the torture of St. Catherine. No, it is not that the world is rubbish and that we throw it away. It is exactly when the whole world of stars is a jewel, like the jewels we have lost, that we remember the price. And we look up as you say, in this dim thicket and see the price, which was the death of God.'

After a silence he added, like one in a dream: 'And the death of man. We shall return by this way to-night.'

Drake had the best reason for being aware of the direction in which their way was now taking them. The familiar path scrambled up the hill to a familiar hedge of juniper, behind which rose the steep roof of a dark mansion. He could even hear voices talking on the lawn behind the hedge, and a note or two of one which changed the current of his blood. He stopped and said in a voice heavy as stone:

'I cannot go in here now. Not for the world.'

'Very well,' replied Father Stephen calmly. 'I think you have waited outside before now.'

And he composedly entered the garden by a gate in the hedge, leaving Drake gloomily kicking his heels on the ledge or natural terrace outside, where he had often waited in happier times. As he did so he could not help hearing fragments of the distant conversation in the garden; and they filled him with confusion and conjecture, not, however, unmingled with hope. It seemed probable that Father Stephen was stating Drake's case and probably offering to prove his innocence. But he must also have been making a sort of appointment, for Drake heard Woodville say: 'I can't make head or tail of this, but we will follow later if you insist.' And Stephen replied with something ending with 'the cross in half an hour.'

Then Drake heard the voice of the girl saying: 'I shall pray to God that you may yet tell us better news.'

'You will be told,' said Father Stephen.

As they redescended towards the little hill just in front of the crucifix, Drake was in a less mutinous mood; whether this was due to the hermit's speech or the words about prayer that had fallen from the woman in the garden. The sky was at once clearer and cloudier than in the previous sunset, for the light and darkness seemed divided by deeper abysses; grey and purple cloudlands as large as landscapes now overcasting the whole earth and now falling again before fresh chasms of light; vast changes that gave to a few hours of evening something of the enormous revolutions of the nights and days. The wall of cloud was then rising higher on the heights behind them and spreading over the château, but the western half of heaven was a clear gold, where the lonely cross stood dark against it. But as they drew nearer they saw that it was in truth less lonely, for a man was standing beneath it. Drake saw a long gun aslant on his back; it was the bearded man of the sabre.

The hermit strode towards him with a strange energy and struck him on the shoulder with the flat of his hand.

'Go home,' he said, 'and tell your masters that their plot will work no longer. If you are Christians, and ever had any part in a holy relic, or any right to it in your land beyond the hills, you will know you should not seek it by such tricks. Go in peace.'

Drake hardly noticed how quickly the man vanished this time, for his eye was fixed on the hermit's finger which seemed idly tracing patterns on the wooden pedestal of the cross. It was really pointing to certain perforations like holes made by worms in the wood.

'Some of the Abbot's stray shots, I think,' he remarked. 'And somebody has been picking them out of the wood strangely enough.'

'It is unlucky,' observed Drake, 'that the Abbot should damage one of your own images; he is as much devoted to the relic as to the realm.'

'More,' said the hermit, sitting down on the knoll a few yards before the pedestal. 'The Abbot, as you truly say, has only room for one ideal in his mind. But there is no doubt of his concern about the stones.'

A great canopy of cloud had again covered the valley, turning twilight almost to darkness; and Stephen spoke out of the dark.

'As for the realm, the Abbot comes from the country beyond the hills, which hundreds of years ago went to war about –'

His words were lost in a distant explosion. A volley had been fired from the tower.

With the first shock of sound Stephen sprang up and stood erect on the little hillock. The world had grown so dark that his attitude could hardly be seen, but as minute followed minute in the interval of silence, a low red light was again gradually released from the drifting cloud, faintly tracing his grey figure in silver and turning his tawny hair to a ring of dim crimson. He was standing quite rigid with his arms stretched out, like a shadow of the crucifix. Drake was striving with the words of a question that would not come. And there then came anew a noise of death from the tower; and the hermit fell all his length crashing among the undergrowth, and lay still as a stone.

Drake hardly knew how he lifted the head on to the wooden pedestal; but the face gave ghastly assurance, and the voice in the few words it could speak was like the voice of a new-born child, weak and small.

'I am dying,' said Father Stephen. 'I am dying with the truth in my heart.'

He made another effort to speak, beginning 'I wish –' and then his friend, looking at him steadily, saw that he was dead.

Bertram Drake stood up, and all his universe lay in ruins around him. The night of annihilation was more absolute because a match had flamed and gone out before it could light the lamp. He was certain now that Stephen had indeed discovered the truth that could deliver him. He was as clearly certain that no other man would ever discover it. He would go blasted to his grave because his friend had died only a moment too soon. And to put a final touch to the hideous irony, that had lifted him to heaven and cast him down, he heard the voices of his friends coming along the road from the château.

In a sort of tumbled dream he saw Dr. Amiel lift the body on to the pedestal, producing surgical instruments for the last hopeless surgical tests. The doctor had his back to Drake, who did not trouble to look over his shoulder, but stared at the ground until the doctor said:

'I fear he is quite dead. But I have extracted the bullet.'

There was something odd about his quiet voice, and the group seemed suddenly, if silently, seething with new emotions. The girl gave an exclamation of wonder, and it seemed of joy, which Drake could not comprehend.

'I am glad I extracted the bullet,' said Dr. Amiel. 'I fancy that's what Drake's friend with the sabre was trying to extract.'

'We certainly owe Drake a complete apology,' observed Woodville.

Drake thrust his head over the other's shoulder, and saw what they were all staring at. The shot that had struck Stephen in the heart lay a few inches from his body, and it not only glittered but sparkled. It sparkled as only one stone can sparkle in the world.

The girl was standing beside him and he appreciated, through the turmoil, the sense of an obstacle rolled away and of a growth and future, and even in all those growing woods the promise of the spring. It was only as the tail of a trailing and vanishing nightmare that he appreciated at last the wild tale of the treason of the foreign Abbot from beyond the hills, and in what strange fashion he loaded his large-mouthed gun. But he continued to gaze at the dazzling speck on the pedestal and saw in it as in a mirror all the past works of his friend.

For Stephen the hermit had died indeed with the truth in his heart; and the truth had been taken out of his heart by the forceps of a wandering Jew; and it lay there on the pedestal of the cross, like the soul drawn out of his body. Nor did it seem unnatural, to the man staring at it, that the soul looked like a star.

6

THE PURPLE JEWEL

Gabriel Gale was a painter and poet; he was the last person to pretend to be even a very private detective. It happened that he had solved several mysteries; but most of them were the sort of mysteries more attractive to a mystic. Nevertheless, it also happened once or twice that he had to step out of the clouds of mysticism into the more brisk and bracing atmosphere of murder. Sometimes he succeeded in showing that a murder was a suicide, sometimes that a suicide was a murder; sometimes he was even involved in the study of lighter occupations like forgery and fraud. But the connection was generally a coincidence; it concerned some point at which his imaginative interest in men's strange motives and moods happened to lead him, or at any rate them, across the border-line of legality. And in most cases, as he himself pointed out, the motives of murderers and thieves are perfectly sane and even conventional.

'I am no good at such a sensible job,' he would say. 'The police could easily make me look a fool in any practical manner such as they discuss in detective stories. What is the good of asking me to measure the marks made by somebody's feet all over the ground, to show why he was walking about, or where he was going? If you will show me the marks of somebody's hands all over the ground, I will tell you why he was walking upside down. But I shall find it out in the only way I ever do find out anything. And this is simply because I am mad, too, and often do it myself.'

A similar brotherhood in folly probably led him into the very baffling mystery of the disappearance of Phineas Salt, the famous author and dramatist. Some of the parties involved may have accepted the parallel of setting a thief to catch a thief, when they set a poet to find a poet. For the problem did involve, in all probability, some of the purely poetical motives of a poet. And even practical people admitted that these might possibly be more familiar to a poet than to a policeman.

Phineas Salt was the sort of man whose private life was rather a public life; like that of Byron or d'Annunzio. He was a remarkable man, and perhaps rather remarkable than respectable. But there was much to be really admired in him; and there were of course any number of people who admired even what was not so admirable. The pessimistic critics claimed him as a great pessimist; and this was widely quoted in support of the theory that his disappearance was in fact a suicide. But the optimistic critics had always obstinately maintained that he was a True Optimist (whatever that may be) and these in their natural rosy rapture of optimism, dwelt rather on the idea that he had been murdered. So lurid and romantic had his whole career been made in the eyes of all Europe, that very few people kept their heads enough to reflect, or summoned their courage to suggest, that there is no particular principle in the nature of things to prevent a great poet falling down a well or being attacked by cramp while swimming at Felixstowe. Most of his admirers, and all those who were by profession journalists, preferred more sublime solutions.

He left no family, of the regular sort, except a brother in a small commercial way in the Midlands, with whom he had had very little to do; but he left a number of other people who stood to him in conspicuous spiritual or economic relations. He left a publisher, whose emotions were of mingled grief and hope in the cessation of his production of books and the high-class advertisement given to those already produced. The publisher was himself a man of considerable social distinction, as such distinctions go to-day; a certain Sir Walter Drummond, the head of a famous and well-established firm; and a type of certain kind of successful Scotchman who contradicts the common tradition by combining being business-like with being extremely radiant and benevolent. He left a theatrical manager in the very act of launching his great poetical play about Alexander and the

Persians; this was an artistic but adaptable Jew, named Isidore Marx, who was similarly balanced between the advantages and disadvantages of an inevitable silence following the cry of 'Author.' He left a beautiful but exceedingly bad-tempered leading actress, who was about to gain fresh glory in the part of the Persian Princess; and who was one of the persons, not indeed few, with whom (as the quaint phrase goes) his name had been connected. He left a number of literary friends; some at least of whom were really literary and a few of whom had really been friendly. But his career had been itself so much like a sensational drama on the stage that it was surprising, when it came to real calculations about his probable conduct, how little anybody seemed to know about the essentials of his real character. And without any such clue, the circumstances seemed to make the poet's absence as disturbing and revolutionary as his presence.

Gabriel Gale, who also moved in the best literary circles, knew all this side of Phineas Salt well enough. He also had been in literary negotiations with Sir Walter Drummond. He also had been approached for poetical plays by Mr. Isidore Marx. He had managed to avoid having 'his name connected' with Miss Hertha Hathaway, the great Shakespearean actress; but he knew her well enough, in a world where everybody knows everybody. But being somewhat carelessly familiar with these noisy outer courts of the fame of Phineas, it gave him a mild shock of irony to pass into the more private and prosaic interior. He owed his connection with the case, not to this general knowledge he shared with the world of letters, but to the accident that his friend, Dr. Garth, had been the family physician of the Salts. And he could not but be amused, when he attended a sort of family council of the matter, to discover how very domestic and even undistinguished the family council was; and how different from the atmosphere of large rumour and loose reputation that roared like a great wind without. He had to remind himself that it is only natural, after all, that anybody's private affairs should be private. It was absurd to expect that a wild poet would have a wild solicitor or a strange and fantastic doctor or dentist. But

Dr. Garth, in the very professional black suit he always wore, looked such a very family physician. The solicitor looked such a very family solicitor. He was a square-faced, silver-haired gentlemen named Gunter; it seemed impossible that his tidy, legal files and strong-boxes could contain such material as the prolonged scandal of Phineas Salt. Joseph Salt, the brother of Phineas Salt, come up specially from the provinces, seemed so very provincial. It was hard to believe that this silent, sandy-haired, big, embarrassed tradesman, in his awkward clothes, was the one other remaining representative of such a name. The party was completed by Salt's secretary, who also seemed disconcertingly secretarial to be closely connected with such an incalculable character. Again Gale had to remind himself that even poets can only go mad on condition that a good many people connected with them remain sane. He reflected, with a faint and dawning interest, that Byron probably had a butler; and possibly even a good butler. The disconnected fancy crossed his mind that even Shelley may have gone to the dentist. He also reflected that Shelley's dentist was probably rather like any other dentist.

Nevertheless, he did not lose the sense of contrast in stepping into this inner chamber of immediate and practical responsibilities. He felt rather out of place in it; for he had no illusions about himself as a business adviser, or one to settle things with the private secretary and the family lawyer. Garth had asked him to come and he sat patiently looking at Garth; while Gunter, the solicitor, laid the general state of things before the informal committee.

'Mr. Hatt has been telling us,' said the lawyer, glancing for a moment at the secretary who sat opposite, 'that he last saw Mr. Phineas Salt at his own flat two hours after lunch on Friday last. Until about an hour ago, I should have said that this interview (which was apparently very short) was the last occasion on which the missing man had been seen. Rather more than an hour ago, however, I was rung up be a person, a complete stranger to me, who declared that he had been with Phineas Salt for the six or seven hours following on that meeting at the flat and that he was coming round to this office as soon as possible, to lay all the facts before us. This evidence, if we find it in any way worthy of credit, will at least carry the story a considerable stage further and perhaps provide us with some important hint about Mr. Salt's whereabouts or fate. I do not think we can say much more about it until he comes.'

'I rather fancy he has come,' said Dr. Garth. 'I heard somebody answering the door; and that sounds like boots scaling these steep legal stairs'; for they had met in the solicitor's office in Lincoln's Inn.

The next moment a slim, middle-aged man slipped rather than stepped into the room; there was indeed something smooth and unobtrusive about the very look of his quiet grey suit, at once shabby and shiny and yet carrying something like the last glimmer of satin and elegance. The only other seizable thing about him was that he not only had rather long hair parted down the middle, but his long olive face was fringed with a narrow dark beard, which was also parted in the middle, drooping in two separated strands. But as he entered he laid on a chair a soft black hat with a very large brim and a very low crown; which somehow called up instantly to the fancy the cafés and the coloured lights of Paris.

'My name is James Florence,' he said in a cultivated accent. 'I was a very old friend of Phineas Salt; and in our younger days I have often travelled about Europe with him. I have every reason to believe that I travelled with him on his last journey.'

'His last journey,' repeated the lawyer, looking at him with frowning attention' 'are you prepared to say that Mr. Salt is dead, or are you saying this for sensationalism?'

'Well, he is either dead or something still more sensational,' said Mr. James Florence.

'What do you mean?' asked the other sharply. 'What could be more sensational than his death?

The stranger looked at him with a fixed and very grave expression and then said simply, 'I cannot imagine.'

Then, when the lawyer made an angry movement, as if

suspecting a joke, the man added equally gravely, 'I am still trying to imagine.'

'Well,' said Gunter, after a pause, 'perhaps you had better tell your story and we will put the conversation on a regular footing. As you probably know, I am Mr. Salt's legal adviser; this is his brother, Mr. Joseph Salt, whom I am advising also; this is Dr. Garth, his medical adviser. This is Mr. Gabriel Gale.'

The stranger bowed to the company and took a seat with quiet confidence.

'I called on my old friend Salt last Friday afternoon about five o'clock. I think I saw this gentleman leaving the flat as I came in.' He looked across at the secretary, Mr. Hatt, a hard-faced and reticent man, who concealed with characteristic discretion, the American name of Hiram; but could not quite conceal a certain American keenness about the look of his long chin and his spectacles. He regarded the newcomer with a face of wood, and said nothing as usual.

'When I entered the flat, I found Phineas in a very disordered and even violent condition, even for him. In fact somebody seemed to have been breaking the furniture; a statuette was knocked off its pedestal and a bowl of irises upset; and he was striding up and down the room like a roaring lion with his red mane rampant and his beard a bonfire. I thought it might be merely an artistic mood, a fine shade of poetical feeling; but he told me he had been entertaining a lady. Miss Hertha Hathaway, the actress, had only just left.

'Here, wait a minute,' interposed the solicitor. 'It would appear that Mr. Hatt, the secretary, had also only just left. But I don't think you said anything about a lady, Mr. Hatt.'

'It's a pretty safe rule,' said the impenetrable Hiram. 'You never asked me about any lady. I've got my own work to do and I told you how I left when I'd done it.'

'This is rather important, though,' said Gunter doubtfully. 'If Salt and the actress threw bowls and statues at each other – well, I suppose we may cautiously conclude there was some slight difference of opinion.'

'There was a final smash-up,' said Florence frankly. 'Phineas told me he was through with all that sort of thing and, as far as I could make out, with everything else as well. He was in a pretty wild state; I think he had been drinking a little already; then he routed out a dusty old bottle of absinthe and said that he and I must drink again in memory of old days in Paris; for it was the last time, or the last day, or some expression of that sort. Well, I hadn't drunk it myself for a long time; but I knew enough about it to know that he was drinking a great deal too much, and it's not a thing like ordinary wine or brandy; the state it can get you into is quite extraordinary; more like the clear madness that comes from hashish. And he finally rushed out of the house with that green fire in his brain and began to get out his car; starting it quite correctly and even driving it well, for there is a lucidity in such intoxication; but driving it faster and faster down the dreary vistas of the Old Kent Road and out into the country towards the south-east. He had dragged me with him with the same sort of hypnotic energy and uncanny conviviality; but I confess I felt pretty uncomfortable spinning out along the country roads with twilight turning to dark. We were nearly killed several times; but I don't think he was trying to be killed – at least not there on the road by an ordinary motor accident. For he kept on crying out that he wanted the high and perilous places of the earth; peaks and precipices and towers; that he would like to take his last leap from some such pinnacle and either fly like an eagle or fall like a stone. And all that seemed the more blind and grotesque because we were driving further and further into some of the flattest country in England, where he certainly would never find any mountains such as towered and toppled in his dream. And then, after I don't know how many hours, he gave a new sort of cry; and I saw, against the last grey strip of the gloaming and all the flat land towards the east, the towers of Canterbury.'

'I wonder,' said Gabriel Gale suddenly, like a man coming out of a dream, 'how they did upset the statuette. Surely the woman threw it, if anybody did. He'd hardly have done a thing like that, even if he was drunk.'

Then he turned his head slowly and stared rather blankly at

the equally blank face of Mr. Hatt; but he said no more and, after a slightly impatient silence, the man called Florence went on with his narrative.

'Of course I knew that the moment he saw the great Gothic towers of the cathedral they would mingle with his waking nightmare and in a way fulfil and crown it. I cannot say whether he had taken that road in order to reach the cathedral; or whether it was merely a coincidence; but there was naturally nothing else in all that landscape that could so fit in with his mood about steep places and dizzy heights. And so of course he took up his crazy parable again and talked about riding upon gargoyles, as upon demon horses, or hunting with hell-hounds above the winds of heaven. It was very late before we reached the cathedral; and though it stands more deeply embedded in the town than is common in cathedral cities, it so happened that the houses nearest to us were all barred and silent and we stood in a deep angle of the building, which had something of seclusion and was covered with the vast shadow of the tower. For a strong moon was already brightening behind the cathedral and I remember the light of it made a sort of ring in Salt's ragged red hair like a dull crimson fire. It seemed a rather unholy halo; and it is a detail I remember the more, because he himself was declaiming in praise of moonshine and especially of the effect of stained-glass windows seen against the moon rather than the sun, as in the famous lines in Keats. He was wild to get inside the building and see the coloured glass, which he swore was the only really successful thing religion ever did; and when he found the cathedral was locked up (as was not unusual at that hour) he had a grand final reaction of rage and scorn and began to curse the dean and chapter and everyone else. Then a blast of boyish historical reminiscence seemed to sweep through his changing mind; and he caught up a great ragged stone from the border of the turf and struck thunderous blows on the door with it, as with a hammer, and shouted aloud, 'King's men! King's men! Where is the traitor? We have come to kill the archbishop.' Then he laughed groggily and said, 'Fancy killing Dr. Randall Davidson . . . But Becket was really worth killing.

He had lived, by God! He had really made the best of both worlds, in a bigger sense than they use the phrase for. Not both at once and both tamely, as the snobs do. But one at a time and both wildly and to the limit. He went clad in crimson and gold and gained laurels and overthrew great knights in tournaments; and then suddenly became a saint, giving his goods to the poor, fasting, dying a martyr. Ah, that is the right way to do it! The right way to live a Double Life! No wonder miracles were worked at his tomb.' Then he hurled the heavy flint from him: and suddenly all the laughter and historical rant seemed to die out of his face and to leave it rather sad and sober; and as stony as one of the stone faces carved above the Gothic doors. 'I shall have to work a miracle to-night,' he said stolidly, 'after I have died.'

'I asked him what in the world he meant; and he made no answer. But he began abruptly to talk to me in quite a quiet and friendly and even affectionate way; thanking me for my companionship on this and many occasions; and saying that we must part; for his time was come. But when I asked him where he was going, he only pointed a finger upwards; and I could not make out at all whether he meant metaphorically that he was going to heaven or materially that he was going to scale the high tower. Anyhow, the only stairway for scaling it was inside and I could not imagine how he could reach it. I tried to question him and he answered, 'I shall ascend . . . ; I shall be lifted up . . . but no miracles will be worked at my tomb. For my body will never be found.'

'And then, before I could move, and without a gesture of warning, he leapt up and caught a stone bracket by the gateway' in another second he was astride it; in a third standing on it; and in a fourth vanished utterly in the vast shadow of the wall above. Once again I heard his voice, much higher up and even far away, crying, 'I shall ascend.' Then all was silence and solitude. I cannot undertake to say whether he did ascend. I can only say with tolerable certainty that he did not descend.'

'You mean,' said Gunter gravely, 'that you have never seen him since.'

'I mean,' answered James Florence equally gravely, 'that I doubt whether anybody on earth has seen him since.'

'Did you make inquiries on the spot?' pursued the lawyer.

The man called Florence laughed in a rather embarrassed fashion. 'The truth is,' he said, 'that I knocked up the neighbours and even questioned the police; and I couldn't get anybody to believe me. They said I had had something to drink, which was true enough; and I think they fancied I had seen myself double, and was trying to chase my own shadow over the cathedral roofs. I daresay they know better now there has been a hue and cry in the newspapers. As for me, I took the last train back to London.'

'What about the car?' asked Garth, sharply; and a light of wonder or consternation came over the stranger's face.

'Why, hang it all!' he cried, 'I forgot all about poor Salt's car! We left it backed into a crack between two old houses just by the cathedral. I never thought of it again till this minute.'

Gunter got up from his desk and went into the inner room, in which he was heard obscurely telephoning. When he came back, Mr. Florence had already picked up his round black hat in his usual unembarrassed manner and suggested that he had better be going; for he had told all that he knew about the affair. Gunter watched him walking away with an interested expression; as if he were not quite so certain of the last assertion as he would like to be. Then he turned to the rest of the company and said:

'A curious yarn. A very curious yarn. But there's another curious thing you ought to know, that may or may not be connected with it.' For the first time he seemed to take notice of the worthy Joseph Salt, who was present as the nearest surviving relative of the deceased or disappearing person. 'Do you happen to know, Mr. Salt, what was your brother's exact financial position?'

'I don't,' said the provincial shopkeeper shortly, and contrived to convey an infinite degree of distance and distaste. 'Of course you understand, gentlemen, that I'm here to do anything I can for the credit of the family. I wish I could feel quite certain that finding poor Phineas will be for the credit of the family.

He and I hadn't much in common, as you may imagine; and to tell the truth, all these newspaper stories don't do a man like me very much good. Men may admire a poet for drinking green fire or trying to fly from a church tower; but they don't order their lunch from a pastry-cook's shop kept by his brother; they get a fancy there might be a little too much green fire in the ginger-ale. And I've only just opened my shop in Croydon; that is, I've bought a new business there. Also,' and he looked down at the table with an embarrassment rather rustic but not unmanly, 'I'm engaged to be married; and the young lady is very active in church work.'

Garth could not suppress a smile at the incongruous lives of the two brothers; but he saw that there was after all, a good deal of common sense in the more obscure brother's attitude.

'Yes,' he said, 'I quite see that; but you can hardly expect the public not to be interested.'

'The question I wanted to ask,' said the solicitor, 'has a direct bearing on something I have just discovered. Have you any notion, even a vague one, of what Phineas Salt's income was, or if he had any capital?'

'Well,' said Joseph Salt reflectively, 'I don't think he really had much capital; he may have had the five thousand we each of us got from the old Dad's business. In fact, I think he had; but I think he lived up to the edge of his income and a bit beyond. He sometimes made big scoops on a successful play or so; but you know the sort of fellow he was; and the big scoop went in a big splash. I should guess he had two or three thousand in the bank when he disappeared.'

'Quite so.' said the solicitor gravely. 'He had two thousand five hundred in the bank on the day he disappeared. And he drew it all out on the day he disappeared. And it entirely disappeared on the day he disappeared.'

'Do you think he's bolted to foreign climes or something?' asked the brother.

'Ah,' answered the lawyer, 'he may have done so. Or he may have intended to do so and not done so.'

'Then how did the money disappear?' asked Garth.

'It may have disappeared,' replied Gunter, 'while Phineas was drunk and talking nonsense to a rather shady Bohemian acquaintance, with a remarkable gift of narration.'

Garth and Gale both glanced sharply across at the speaker; and both, observant in such different ways, realized that the lawyer's face was a shade too grim to be called merely cynical.

'Ah,' cried the doctor with something like a catch in his breath. 'And you mean something worse than theft.'

'I have no right to assert even theft.' said the lawyer, without relaxing his sombre expression, 'but I have a right to suspect things that go rather deep. To begin with, there is some evidence for the start of Mr. Florence's story, but none for its conclusion. Mr. Florence met Mr. Hatt; I take it, from the absence of contradiction, that Mr. Hatt also met Mr. Florence.'

On the poker face of Mr. Hatt there was still an absence of contradiction; that might presumably be taken for confirmation.

'Indeed, I have found some evidence corroborating the story of Salt starting with Florence in the car. There is no evidence corroborating all that wild moonlight antic on the roads of Kent; and if you ask me, I think it very likely that this particular joy-ride ended in some criminal den in the Old Kent Road. I telephoned a moment ago to ask about the car left in Canterbury; and they cannot at present find traces of any such car. Above all, there is the damning fact that this fellow Florence forgot all about his imaginary car, and contradicted himself by saying that he went back by train. That alone makes me think his story is false.'

'Does it?' asked Gale, looking at him with childlike wonder. 'Why, that alone makes me think his story is true.'

'How do you mean?' asked Gunter, 'that alone?'

'Yes,' said Gale; 'that one detail is so true that I could almost believe the truth of all the rest, if he'd described Phineas as flying from the tower on a stone dragon.'

He sat frowning and blinking for a moment and then said rather testily, 'Don't you see it's just the sort of mistake that would be made by that sort of man? A shabby, impecunious man, a man who never travels far except in trains, is caught up for one wild ride in a rich friend's car, drugged into a sort of dream of absinthe, dragged into a topsy-turvy mystery like a nightmare, wakes up to find his friend caught up into the sky and everybody, in broad daylight, denying that the thing had ever happened. In that sort of chilly, empty awakening, a poor man talking to a contemptuous policeman, he would no more have remembered any responsibility for the car than if it had been a fairy chariot drawn by griffins. It was part of the dream. He would automatically fall back on his ordinary way of life and take a third-class ticket home. But he would never make such a blunder in a story he had entirely made up for himself. The instant I heard him make that howler, I knew he was telling the truth.'

The others were gazing at the speaker in some mild surprise, when the telephone bell, strident and prolonged, rang in the adjoining office. Gunter got hastily to his feet and went to answer it. and for a few moments there was no sound but the faint buzz of his questions and replies. Then he came back into the room, his strong face graven with a restrained stupefaction.

'This is a most remarkable coincidence,' he said; 'and, I must admit, a confirmation of what you say. The police down there have found the marks of a car, with tyres and general proportions like Phineas Salt's, evidently having stood exactly where James Florence professed to have left it standing. But what is even more odd, it has gone; the tracks show it was driven off down the road to the south-east by somebody. Presumably by Phineas Salt.'

'To the south-east,' cried Gale, and sprang to his feet. 'I thought so!'

He took a few strides up and down the room and then said, 'But we mustn't go too fast. There are several things. To begin with, any fool can see that Phineas would drive to the east; it was nearly daybreak when he disappeared. Of course, in that state, he would drive straight into the sunrise. What else could one do? Then, if he was really full of that craze for crags or towers, he would find himself leaving the last towers behind and driving into flatter and flatter places; for that road leads into Thanet. What would he do? He must make for the chalk cliffs that look down at least on sea and sand; but I fancy he would want to look down on people too; just as he might have looked down on the people of Canterbury from the cathedral tower. . . . I know that south-eastern road. . . .'

Then he faced them solemnly and, like one uttering a sacred mystery, said, 'Margate.'

'And why?' asked the staring Garth.

'A form of suicide, I suppose,' said the solicitor dryly. 'What could a man of that sort want to do at Margate except commit suicide?'

'What could any man want at Margate except suicide?' asked Dr. Garth, who had a prejudice against such social resorts.

'A good many millions of God's images go there simply for fun,' said Gale; 'but it remains to be shown why one of them should be Phineas Salt . . . there are possibilities . . . those blank crawling masses seen from the white cliffs might be a sort of vision for a pessimist; possibly a dreadful destructive vision of shutting the gates in the cliffs and inundating them all in the ancient awful sea . . . or could he have some cranky notion of making Margate glorious by his creative or destructive acts; changing the very sound of the name, making it heroic or tragic for ever? There have been such notions in such men . . . but wherever this wild road leads I am sure it ends in Margate.'

The worthy tradesman of Croydon was the first to get to his feet after Gale had risen, and he fingered the lapels of his outlandish coat with all his native embarrassment. 'I'm afraid all this is beyond me, gentlemen,' he said, 'gargoyles and dragons and pessimists and such are not in my line. But it does seem that the police have got a clue that points down the Margate road; and if you ask me, I think we'd better discuss this matter again when the police have investigated a little more.'

'Mr. Salt is perfectly right,' said the lawyer heartily. 'See what it is to have a business man to bring us back to business. I will go and make some more inquiries; and soon, perhaps, I may have a little more to tell you.'

If Gabriel Gale was, and felt himself to be, an incongruous

figure in the severe framework of leather and parchment, of law and commerce, represented by the office of Mr Gunter, it might well have been supposed that he would feel even more of a fish out of water in the scene of the second family council. For it was held at the new headquarters of the family, or all that remained of the family; the little shop in Croydon over which the lost poet's very prosaic brother was presiding with a mixture of the bustle of a new business and the last lingering formalities of a funeral. Mr. J. Salt's suburban shop was a very suburban shop. It was a shop for selling confectionery and sweetmeats and similar things; with a sort of side-show of very mild refreshments, served on little round shiny tables and apparently chiefly consisting of pale green lemonade. The cakes and sweets were arranged in decorative patterns in the window, to attract the eye of Croydon youth, and as the building consisted chiefly of windows, it seemed full of a sort of cold and discolouring light. A parlour behind, full of neat but illogical knickknacks and mementoes, was not without a sampler, a testimonial from a Provident Society and a portrait of George V. But it was never easy to predict in what place or circumstances Mr. Gale would find a certain intellectual interest. He generally looked at objects, not objectively in the sense of seeing them as themselves, but in connection with some curious trains of thought of his own; and, for some reason or other, he seemed to take quite a friendly interest in Mr. Salt's suburban shop. Indeed, he seemed to take more interest in this novel scene than in the older and more serious problem which he had come there to solve. He gazed entranced at the china dogs and pink pincushions on the parlour mantelpiece; he was with difficulty drawn away from a rapt contemplation of the diamond pattern of lemon-drops and raspberry-drops which decorated the window; and he looked even at the lemonade as if it were as important as that pale green wine of wormwood, which had apparently played a real part in the tragedy of Phineas Salt.

He had been indeed unusually cheerful all the morning, possibly because it was a beautiful day, possibly for more personal reasons; and had drawn near to the rendezvous through the trim suburban avenues with a step of unusual animation. He saw the worthy confectioner himself, stepping out of a villa of a social shade faintly superior to his own; a young woman with a crown of braided brown hair, and a good grave face, came with him down the garden path. Gale had little difficulty in identifying the young lady interested in church work. The poet gazed at the pale squares of lawn and the few thin and dwarfish trees with quite a sentimental interest, almost as if it were a romance of his own; nor did his universal good humour fail him when he encountered, a few lamp-posts further down the road, the saturnine and somewhat unsympathetic countenance of Mr. Hiram Hatt. The lover was still lingering at the garden gate, after the fashion of his kind, and Hatt and Gale walked more briskly ahead of him towards his home. To Hatt the poet made the somewhat irrelevant remark, 'Do you understand that desire to be one of the lovers of Cleopatra?'

Mr. Hatt, the secretary, indicated that, had he nourished such a desire, his appearance on the historical scene would have lacked something of true American hustle and punctuality.

'Oh, there are plenty of Cleopatras still,' answered Gale; 'and plenty of people who have that strange notion of being the hundredth husband of an Egyptian cat. What could have made a man of real intellect, like that fellow's brother, break himself all up for a woman like Hertha Hathaway?'

'Well, I'm all with you there,' said Hatt. 'I didn't say anything about the woman, because it wasn't my business; but I tell you, sir, she was just blue ruin and vitriol. Only the fact that I didn't mention her seems to have set your friend the solicitor off on another dance of dark suspicion. I swear he fancies she and I were mixed up in something; and probably had to do with the disappearance of Phineas Salt.'

Gale looked hard at the man's hard face for a moment and then said irrelevantly: 'Would it surprise you to find him at Margate?'

'No; nor anywhere else,' replied Hatt. 'He was restless just then and drifted about into the commonest crowds. He did no work lately; sometimes sat and stared at a blank sheet of paper as if he had no ideas.'

'Or as if he had too many,' said Gabriel Gale.

With that they turned in at the confectioner's door; and found Dr. Garth already in the outer shop, having only that moment arrived. But when they penetrated to the parlour, they came on a figure that gave them,indescribably, a cold shock of sobriety. The lawyer was already seated in that gim-crack room, resolutely and rather rudely, with his top hat on his head, like a bailiff in possession; but they all sensed something more sinister, as of the bearer of the bowstring.

'Where is Mr. Joseph Salt?' he asked. 'He said he would be home at eleven.'

Gale smiled faintly and began to fiddle with the funny little ornaments on the mantelpiece. 'He is saying farewell,' he said. 'Sometimes it is rather a long word to say.'

'We must begin without him,' said Gunter. 'Perhaps it is just as well.'

'You mean you have bad news for him?' asked the doctor, lowering his voice. 'Have you the last news of his brother?'

'I believe it may fairly be called the last news,' answered the lawyer dryly. 'In the light of the latest discoveries – Mr. Gale, I should be much obliged if you would leave of fidgeting with those ornaments and sit down. There is something that somebody has got to explain.'

'Yes,' replied Gale rather hazily. 'Isn't *this* what he has got to explain?'

He picked up something from the mantelpiece and put it on the central table. It was a very absurd object to be stared at thus, as an exhibit in a grim museum of suicide or crime. It was a cheap, childish, pink and white mug, inscribed in large purple letters, 'A Present from Margate.'

'There is a date inside,' said Gale, looking down dreamily into the depths of this remarkable receptacle. 'This year. And we're still at the beginning of the year, you know.'

'Well, it may be one of the things,' said the solicitor. 'But I have got some other Presents from Margate.'

He took a sheaf of papers from his breast-pocket and laid them out thoughtfully on the table before he spoke.

'Understand, to begin with, that there really is a riddle and the man really has vanished. Don't imagine a man can easily melt into a modern crowd; the police have traced his car on the road and could have traced him, if he had left it. Don't imagine anybody can simply drive down country roads throwing corpses out of cars. There are always a lot of fussy people about, who notice a little thing like that. Whatever he did, sooner or later the explanation would probably be found; and we have found it.'

Gale put down the mug abruptly and stared across, still open-mouthed, but as it were more dry-throated, coughing and stammering now with a real eagerness.

'Have you really found out?' he asked. 'Do you know all about the Purple Jewel?'

'Look here!' cried the doctor, as with a generous indignation; 'this is getting too thick. I don't mind being in a mystery, but it needn't be a melodrama. Don't say that we are after the Rajah's Ruby. Don't say, oh, don't say, that it is the eye of the god Vishnu.'

'No,' replied the poet. 'It is the eye of the Beholder.'

'And who's he?' asked Gunter. 'I don't know exactly what you're talking about, but there may have been a theft involved. Anyhow, there was more than a theft.'

He sorted out from his papers two or three photographs of the sort that are taken casually with hand cameras in a holiday crowd. As he did so he said:

'Our investigations at Margate have not been fruitless; in fact they have been rather fruitful. We have found a witness, a photographer on Margate beach, who testifies to having seen a man corresponding to Phineas Salt, burly and with a big red beard and long hair, who stood for some time on an isolated crag of white chalk, which stands out from the cliff, and looked down at the crowds below. Then he descended by a rude stairway cut in the chalk and, crossing a crowded part of the beach, spoke to another man who seemed to be an ordinary clerk or commonplace holiday-maker; and, after a little talk, they went up to the row of bathing-sheds, apparently for the purpose of having a dip in the sea. My informant thinks they did go into the sea; but he cannot be quite so certain. What he is quite certain of is that he never saw the red-bearded man again, though he did see the commonplace clean-shaven man, both when he returned in his bathing-suit and when he resumed his ordinary, his very ordinary, clothes. He not only saw him, but he actually took a snapshot of him, and there he is.'

He handed the photograph to Garth, who gazed at it with slowly rising eyebrows. The photograph represented a sturdy man with a bulldog jaw but rather blank eyes, with his head lifted, apparently staring out to sea. He wore very light holiday clothes, but of a clumsy unfashionable cut; and, so far as he could be seen under the abrupt shadow and rather too jaunty angle of his stiff straw hat, his hair was of some light colour. Only, as it happened, the doctor had no need to wait for the development of colour photography. For he knew exactly what colour it was. He knew it was a sort of sandy red; he had often seen it, not in the photograph, but on the head where it grew. For the man in the stiff straw hat was most unmistakably Mr. Joseph Salt, the worthy confectioner and new social ornament to the suburb of Croydon.

'So Phineas went down to Margate to meet his brother,' said Garth. 'After all, that's natural enough in one way. Margate is exactly the sort of place his brother would go to.'

'Yes; Joseph went there on one of those motor-char-à-banc expeditions, with a whole crowd of other trippers, and he seems to have returned the same night on the same vehicle. But nobody knows when, where or *if* his brother Phineas returned.'

'I rather gather from your tone,' said Garth very gravely, 'that you think his brother Phineas never did return.'

'I think his brother never will return,' said the lawyer, 'unless it happens (by a curious coincidence) that he was drowned while bathing and his body is one day washed up on the shore. But there's a strong current running just there that would carry it far away.'

'The plot thickens, certainly,' said the doctor. 'All this bathing business seems to complicate things rather.'

'I am afraid,' said the lawyer, 'that it simplifies them very much.'

'What,' asked Garth sharply. 'Simplifies?'

'Yes,' said the other, gripping the arms of his chair and rising abruptly to his feet. 'I think this story is as simple as the story of Cain and Abel. And rather like it.'

There was a shocked silence, which was at length broken by Gale, who was peering into the Present from Margate, crying or almost crowing, in the manner of a child.

'Isn't it a funny little mug! He must have bought it before he came back in the char-à-banc. Such a jolly thing to buy, when you have just murdered you own brother.'

'It does seem a queer business.' said Dr. Garth, frowning. 'I suppose one might work out some explanation of how he did it. I suppose a man might drown another man while they were bathing, even off a crowded beach like that. But I'm damned if I can understand why he did it. Have you discovered a motive as well as a murder?'

'The motive is old enough and I think obvious enough,' answered Gunter. 'We have in this case all the necessary elements of a hatred, of that slow and corroding sort that is founded on jealousy. Here you had two brothers, sons of the same insignificant Midland tradesman; having the same education, environment, opportunities; very nearly of an age, very much of one type, even of one physical type, rugged, red-haired, rather plain and heavy, until Phineas made himself a spectacle with that big Bolshevist beard and bush of hair; not so different in youth but that they must have had ordinary rivalries and quarrels on fairly equal terms. And then see the sequel. One of them fills the world with his name, wears a laurel like the crown of Petrarch, dines with kings and emperors and is worshipped by women like a hero on the films. The other – isn't it enough to say that the other has had to go on slaving all his life in a room like this?'

'Don't you like the room?' inquired Gale with the same simple eagerness. 'Why, I think some of the ornaments are so nice!'

'It is not yet quite clear,' went on Gunter, ignoring him, 'how the pastry-cook lured the poet down to Margate and a dip in the sea. But the poet was admittedly rather random in his movements just then, and too restless to work; and we have no reason to suppose that he knew of the fraternal hatred or that he in any way reciprocated it. I don't think there would be much difficulty in swimming with a man beyond the crowd of bathers and holding him under the water, till you could send his body adrift on a current flowing away from the shore. Then he went back and dressed and calmly took his place in the char-à-banc.'

'Don't forget the dear little mug,' said Gale softly. 'He stopped to buy that and then went home. Well, it's a very able and thorough explanation and reconstruction of the crime, my dear Gunter, and I congratulate you. Even the best achievements have some little flaw; and there's only one trifling mistake in your. You've got it the wrong way round.'

'What do you mean?' asked the other quickly.

'Quite a small correction,' explained Gale. 'You think that Joseph was jealous of Phineas. As a matter of fact, Phineas was jealous of Joseph.'

'My dear Gale, you are simply playing the goat,' said the doctor very sharply and impatiently. 'And let me tell you I don't think it's a decent occasion for doing it. I know all about your jokes and fancies and paradoxes, but we're all in a damned hard position, sitting here in the man's own house, and knowing we're in the house of a murderer.'

'I know – it's simply infernal,' said Gunter, his stiffness shaken for the first time; and he looked up with a shrinking jerk, as if he half expected to see the rope hanging from that dull and dusty ceiling.

At the same moment the door was thrown open and the man they had convicted of murder stood in the room. His eyes were bright like a child's over a new toy, his face was flushed to the roots of his fiery hair, his broad shoulders were squared backwards like a soldier's; and in the lapel of his coat was a large purple flower, of a colour that Gale remembered in the garden-beds of the house down the road. Gale had no difficulty in guessing the reason of this triumphant entry.

Then the man with the buttonhole saw the tragic faces on the other side of the table and stopped, staring.

'Well,' he said at last, in a rather curious tone. 'What about your search?'

The lawyer was about to open his locked lips with some such question as was once asked of Cain by the voice out of the cloud, when Gale interrupted him by flinging himself backwards in a chair and emitting a short but cheery laugh.

'I've given up the search,' said Gale gaily. 'No need to bother myself about that any more.'

'Because you know you will never find Phineas Salt,' said the tradesman steadily.

'Because I have found him,' said Gabriel Gale.

Dr. Garth got to his feet quickly and remained staring at them with bright eyes.

'Yes,' said Gale, 'because I am talking to him.' And he smiled across at his host, as if he had just been introduced.

Then he said rather more gravely, 'Will you tell us all about it, Mr. Phineas Salt? Or must I guess it for you all the way through?'

There was a heavy silence.

'You tell the story,' said the shopkeeper at last. 'I am quite sure you know all about it.'

'I only know about it,' answered Gale gently, 'because I think I should have done the same thing myself. It's what some call having a sympathy with lunatics – including literary men.'

'Hold on for a moment,' interposed the staring Mr. Gunter. 'Before you get too literary, am I to understand that this gentleman, who owns this shop, actually is the poet, Phineas Salt? In that case, where is his brother?'

'Making the Grand Tour, I imagine,' said Gale. 'Gone abroad for a holiday, anyhow; a holiday which will be not the less enjoyable for the two thousand five hundred pounds that his brother gave him to enjoy himself with. His slipping away was easy enough; he only swam a little bit further along the shore to where they had left another suit of clothes. Meanwhile our friend here went back and shaved off his beard and effected the change of appearance in the bathing-tent. He was quite sufficiently like his brother to go back with a crowd of strangers. And then, you will doubtless note, he opened a new shop in an entirely new neighbourhood.'

'But *why*?' cried Garth in a sort of exasperation. 'In the name of all the saints and angels, why? That's what I can't make any sense of.'

'I will tell you why,' said Gabriel Gale, 'but you won't make any sense of it.'

He stared at the mug on the table for a moment and then said: 'This is what you would call a nonsense story; and you can only understand it by understanding nonsense; or, as some politely call it, poetry. The poet Phineas Salt was a man who had made himself master of everything, in a sort of frenzy of freedom and omnipotence. He had tried to feel everything, experience everything, imagine everything that could be or could not be. And he found, as all such men have found, that illimitable liberty is itself a limit. It is like the circle, which is at once an eternity and a prison. He not only wanted to do everything. He wanted to be everybody. To the Pantheist God is everybody; to the Christian He is also somebody. But this sort of Pantheist will not narrow himself by a choice. To want everything is to will nothing. Mr. Hatt here told me that Phineas would sit staring at a blank sheet of paper; and I told him it was not because he had nothing to write about, but because he could write about anything. When he stood on that cliff and looked down on that mazy crowd, so common and yet so complex, he felt he could write ten thousand tales and then that he could write none; because there was no reason to choose one more than another.

'Well, what is the step beyond that? What comes next? I tell you there are only two steps possible after that. One is the step over the cliff; to cease to be. The other is to *be* somebody, instead of writing about everybody. It is to become incarnate as one real human being in that crowd; to begin all over again as a real person. Unless a man be born again –

'He tried it and found that this was what he wanted; the things he had not known since childhood; the silly little lower middle-class things; to have to do with lollipops and ginger-beer; to fall in love with a girl round the corner and feel awkward about it; to be young. That was the only paradise still left virgin and unspoilt enough, in the imagination of a man who has turned the seven heavens upside down. That is what he tried as his last experiment, and I think we can say it has been a success.'

'Yes.' said the confectioner with a stony satisfaction, 'it has been a great success.'

Mr Gunter, the solicitor, rose also with a sort of gesture of despair. 'Well, I don't think I understand it any better for knowing all about it,' he said; 'but I suppose it must be as you say. But how in the world did you know it yourself?'

'I think it was those coloured sweets in the window that set me off,' said Gale. 'I couldn't take my eyes off them. They were so pretty. Sweets are better than jewelry: the children are right. For they have the fun of eating rubies and emeralds. I felt sure they were speaking to me in some way. And then I realized what they were saying. Those violet or purple raspberry drops were as vivid and glowing as amethysts, when you saw them from *inside* the shop; but from outside, with the light on them, they would look quite dingy and dark. Meanwhile, there were plenty of other things, gilded or painted with opaque colours, that would have looked much more gay in the shop-window, to the customer looking in at it. Then I remembered the man who said he must break into the cathedral to see the coloured windows from inside, and I knew it in an instant. The man who had arranged that shop-window was not a shopkeeper. He was not thinking of how things looked from the street, but of how they looked to his own artistic eye from inside. From there he saw purple jewels. And then, thinking of the cathedral, of course I remembered something else. I remembered what the poet had said about the Double Life of St. Thomas of Canterbury; and how when he had all the earthly glory, he had to have the exact opposite. St. Phineas of Croydon is also living a Double Life.'

'Well,' broke out Gunter, heaving with a sort of heavy gasp, 'with all respect to him, if he has done all this, I can only say that he must have gone mad.'

'No,' said Gale, 'a good many of my friends have gone mad and I am by no means without sympathy with them. But you can call this the story of 'The Man Who Went Sane.' '

7

THE VANISHING PRINCE

This tale begins among the tangle of tales round a name that is at once recent and legendary. The name is that of Michael O'Neill, popularly called Prince Michael; partly because he claimed descent from ancient Fenian princes, and partly because he was credited with a plan to make himself Prince President of Ireland, as the last Napoleon did of France.He was undoubtedly a gentleman of honourable pedigree and of many accomplishments; but two of his accomplishments emerged from all the rest. He had a talent for appearing when he was not wanted, and a talent for disappearing when he was wanted; especially when he was wanted by the police. It may be added that his disappearances were more dangerous than his appearances. In the latter he seldom went beyond the sensational – pasting up seditious placards, tearing down official placards, making flamboyant speeches or unfurling forbidden flags. But in order to effect the former, he would sometimes fight for his freedom with a startling energy, from which men were sometimes lucky to escape with a broken head instead of a broken neck. His most famous feats of escape, however, were due to dexterity and not to violence. On a cloudless summer morning he had come down a country road white with dust, and pausing outside a farmhouse, had told the farmer's daughter, with elegant indifference, that the local police were in pursuit of him. The girl's name was Bridget Royce, a sombre and even sullen type of beauty, and she looked at him darkly, as if in doubt, and said: 'Do you want me to hide you?' Upon which he only laughed, leapt lightly over the stone wall and strode towards the farm, merely throwing over his shoulder the remark: 'Thank you, I have generally been quite capable of hiding myself.' In which proceeding he acted with a tragic ignorance of the nature of women, and there fell on his path in that sunshine a shadow of doom.

While he disappeared through the farmhouse, the girl remained for a few moments looking up the road, and two perspiring policemen came ploughing up to the door where she stood. Though still angry, she was still silent, and a quarter of an hour later the officers had searched the house and were already inspecting the kitchen-garden and cornfield behind it. In the ugly reaction of her mood, she might have been tempted even to point out the fugitive, but for a small difficulty – that she had no more notion than the policemen had of where he could possibly have gone. The kitchen-garden was enclosed by a very low wall and the cornfield beyond lay aslant, like a square patch on a great green hill, on which he could still have been seen even as a dot in the distance. Everything stood solid in its familiar place; the apple-tree was too small to support or hide a climber; the only shed stood open and obviously empty; there was no sound save the droning of summer flies and the occasional flutter of a bird unfamiliar enough to be surprised by the scarecrow in the field; there was scarcely a shadow save a few blue lines that fell from the thin tree; every detail was picked out by the brilliant daylight as if in a microscope. The girl described the scene later, with all the passionate realism of her race; and whether or not the policemen had a similar eye for the picturesque, they had at least an eye for the facts of the case, and were compelled to give up the chase and retire from the scene. Bridget Royce remained, as if in a trance, staring at the sunlit garden in which a man had just vanished like a fairy. She was still in a sinister mood, and the miracle took in her mind a character of unfriendliness and fear, as if the fairy were decidedly a bad fairy. The sun upon the glittering garden depressed her more than darkness, but she continued to stare at it. Then the world itself went half-witted, and she screamed. The scarecrow moved in the sunlight. It had stood with its back to her in a battered, old black hat and a tattered garment, and with all its tatters flying, it strode away across the hill.

She did not analyze the audacious trick by which the man had turned to his advantage the subtle effects of the expected and the obvious; she was still under the cloud of more individual complexities, and she noticed most of all that the vanishing scarecrow did not even turn to look at the farm. And the fates that were running so adverse to his fantastic career of freedom ruled that his next adventure, though it had the same success in another quarter, should increase the danger in this quarter. Among the many similar adventures related of him in this manner, it is also said that some days afterwards another girl, named Mary Cregan, found him concealed on the farm where she worked, and if the story is true, she must also have had the shock of an uncanny experience. For when she was busy at some lonely task in the yard, she heard a voice speaking out of the well, and found that the eccentric had managed to drop himself into the bucket which was some little way below, the well being only partly full of water. In this case, however, he had to appeal to the woman to wind up the rope. And men say it was when this news was told to the other woman, that her soul walked over the border-line of treason.

Such, at least, were the stories told of them in the countryside, and there were many more; as that he had stood insolently in a splendid green dressing-gown on the steps of a great hotel, and then led the police a chase through a long suite of grand apartments, and finally through his own bedroom on to a balcony that overhung the river. The moment the pursuers stepped on to the balcony it broke under them, and they dropped pell-mell into the eddying waters, while Michael, who had thrown off his gown and dived, was able to swim away. It was said that he had carefully cut away the props so that they would not support anything so heavy as a policeman. But here again he was immediately fortunate yet ultimately unfortunate, for it is said that one of the men was drowned, leaving a family feud which made a little rift in his popularity. These stories can now be told in some detail, not because they are the most marvellous of his many adventures, but because these alone were not covered with silence by the loyalty of the peasantry. These alone found their way into official reports, and it is these which three of the chief officials of the country were reading and discussing when the more remarkable part of this story begins.

Night was far advanced, and the lights shone in the cottage that served for a temporary police-station near the coast. On one side of it were the last houses of the straggling village, and on the other nothing but a waste moorland stretching away towards the sea, the line of which was broken by no landmark except a solitary tower, of the prehistoric pattern still found in Ireland, standing up as slender as a column but pointed like a pyramid. At a wooden table, in front of the window which normally looked out on this landscape, sat two men in plain clothes but with something of a military bearing, for, indeed, they were the two chiefs of the detective service of that district. The senior of the two, both in age and rank, was a sturdy man with a short white beard and frosty eyebrows, fixed in a frown which suggested rather worry than severity.

His name was Morton, and he was a Liverpool man long pickled in the Irish quarrels, and doing his duty among them in a sour fashion not altogether unsympathetic. He had spoken a few sentences to his companion Nolan, a tall, dark man with a cadaverous equine Irish face, when he seemed to remember something and touched a bell which rang in another room. The subordinate he had summoned immediately appeared with a sheaf of papers in his hand.

'Sit down, Wilson,' he said. 'Those are the depositions, I suppose.'

'Yes,' replied the third officer. 'I think I've got all there is to be got out of them, so I sent the people away.'

'Did Mary Cregan give evidence?' asked Morton, with a frown that looked a little heavier than usual.

'No, but her master did,' answered the man called Wilson, who had flat red hair and a plain pale face, not without sharpness. 'I think he's hanging round the girl himself and is out against a rival. There's always some reason of that sort when we are told the truth about anything. And you bet the other girl told right enough.'

'Well, let's hope they'll be some sort of use,' remarked Nolan, in a somewhat hopeless manner, gazing out into the darkness.

'Anything is to the good,' said Morton, 'that lets us know anything about him.'

'Do we know anything about him?' asked the melancholy Irishman.

'We know one thing about him.' said Wilson, 'and it's the one thing that nobody ever knew before. We know where he is.'

'Are you sure?' inquired Morton, looking at him sharply.

'Quite sure,' replied his assistant. 'At this very minute he is in that tower over there by the shore. If you go near enough you'll see the candle burning in the window.'

As he spoke the noise of a horn sounded on the road outside, and a moment after they heard the throbbing of a motor-car brought to a standstill before the door. Morton instantly sprang to his feet.

'Thank the Lord, that's the car from Dublin,' he said. 'I can't do anything without special authority, not if he were sitting on the top of the tower and putting out his tongue at us. But the Chief can do what he thinks best.'

He hurried out to the entrance and was soon exchanging greetings with a big, handsome man in a fur coat, who brought into the dingy little station the indescribable glow of the great cities and the luxuries of the great world.

For this was Sir Walter Carey, an official of such eminence in Dublin Castle that nothing short of the case of Prince Michael would have brought him on such a journey in the middle of the night. But the case of Prince Michael, as it happened, was complicated by legalism as well as lawlessness. On the last occasion he had escaped by a forensic quibble and not, as usual, by a private escapade, and it was a question whether, at the moment, he was amenable to the law or not. It might be necessary to stretch a point; but a man like Sir Walter could probably stretch it as far as he liked.

Whether he intended to do so was a question to be considered. Despite the almost aggressive touch of luxury in the fur coat, it soon became apparent that Sir Walter's large leonine head was for use as well as ornament, and he considered the matter soberly and sanely enough. Five chairs were set round the plain deal table, for Sir Walter had brought with him a young relative and secretary named Horne Fisher, a rather languid young man with a light moustache and hair prematurely thinned. Sir Walter listened with grave attention, and his secretary with polite boredom, to the string of episodes by which the police had traced the flying rebel from the steps of the hotel to the solitary tower beside the sea. There, at least, he was cornered between the moors and the breakers, and the scout sent by Wilson reported him as writing under a solitary candle; perhaps composing another of his tremendous proclamations. Indeed it would have been typical of him to have chosen it as the place in which finally to turn to bay. He had some remote claim on it, as on a family castle, and those who knew him thought him capable of imitating the primitive Irish Chieftain, who fell fighting against the sea.

'I saw some queer-looking people leaving as I came in,' said Sir Walter Carey. 'I suppose they were your witnesses. But why do they turn up here at this time of night?'

Morton smiled grimly.

'They come here by night because they would be dead men if they came here by day. They are criminals committing a crime that is more horrible here than theft or murder.'

'What crime do you mean?' asked the other, with some curiosity.

'They are helping the law,' said Morton.

There was a silence, and Sir Walter considered the papers before him with an abstracted eye. At last he spoke.

'Quite so; but look here, if the local feeling is as lively as that, there are a good many points to consider. I believe the new Act will enable me to collar him now if I think it best. But is it best? A serious rising here would do us no good in Parliament, and the Government has enemies in England as well as Ireland. It won't do if I have done what looks a little like sharp practice, and then only raised a revolution.'

'It's all the other way,' said the man called Wilson, rather quickly. 'There won't be half so much of a revolution if you arrest him as there will if you leave him loose for three days longer. But, anyhow, there can't be anything nowadays that the proper police can't manage.'

'Mr. Wilson is a Londoner,' said the Irish detective, with a smile.

'Yes, I'm a Cockney all right,' replied Wilson, 'and I think I'm all the better for that. Especially at this job, oddly enough.'

Sir Walter seemed slightly amused at the pertinacity of the third officer, and perhaps even more amused at the slight accent with which he spoke, which rendered rather needless his boast about his origin.

'Do you mean to say,' he asked, 'that you know more about the business here because you have come from London?'

'Sounds funny, I know, but I do believe it,' answered Wilson. 'I believe these affairs want fresh methods. But most of all I believe they want a fresh eye.'

The superior officers laughed, and the red-haired man went on with a slight touch of temper.

'Well, look at the facts. See how the fellow got away every time, and you'll understand what I mean. Why was he able to stand in the place of the scarecrow, hidden by nothing but an old hat? Because it was a village policeman who knew the scarecrow was there – expecting it, and therefore took no notice of it. Now I never expect a scarecrow. I've never seen one in the street, and I stare at one when I see it in the field. It's a new thing to me, and worth noticing. And it was just the same when he hid in the well. You are ready to find a well in a place like that; you look for a well, and so you don't see it. I don't look for it, and therefore I do look at it.'

'It is certainly an idea,' said Sir Walter, smiling. 'But what about the balcony? Balconies are occasionally seen in London.'

'But not rivers right under them, as if it was in Venice,' replied Wilson.

'It is certainly a new idea,' repeated Sir Walter, with something like respect. He had all the love of the luxurious classes for new ideas. But he also had a critical faculty, and was inclined to think, after due reflection, that it was a true idea as well.

Growing dawn had already turned the window panes from black to grey, when Sir Walter got abruptly to his feet. The others rose also, taking this for a signal that the arrest was to be undertaken. But their leader stood for a moment in deep thought, as if conscious that he had come to a parting of the ways.

Suddenly the silence was pierced by a long, wailing cry from the dark moors outside. The silence that followed it seemed more startling than the shriek itself, and it lasted until Nolan said heavily:

' 'Tis the banshee. Somebody is marked for the grave.'

His long, large-featured face was as pale as a moon; and it was easy to remember that he was the only Irishman in the room

'Well, I know that banshee,' said Wilson, cheerfully. 'Ignorant as you think I am of these things. I talked to that banshee myself an hour ago, and I sent that banshee up to the tower and told her to sing out like that, if she could get a glimpse of our friend writing his proclamation.'

'Do you mean that girl Bridget Royce?' asked Morton, drawing his frosty brows together. 'Has she turned King's evidence to that extent?'

'Yes,' said Wilson. 'I know very little of these local things, you will tell me. But I reckon an angry woman is much the same in all countries.'

Nolan, however, seemed still moody and unlike himself.

'It's an ugly noise and an ugly business altogether,' he said. 'If it's really the end of Prince Michael, it may well be the end of other things as well. When the spirit is on him he would escape by a ladder of dead men, and wade through that sea if it were made of blood.'

'Is that the real reason of your pious alarms?' asked Wilson, with a slight sneer.

The Irishman's pale face blackened with a new passion.

'I have faced as many murderers in County Clare as you ever fought with in Clapham Junction, Mr. Cockney,' he said.

'Hush please,' said Morton sharply. 'Wilson, you have no kind of right to imply doubt of your superior's conduct. I hope you will prove yourself as courageous and trustworthy as he has always been.'

The pale face of the red-haired man seemed a shade paler, but he was silent and composed, and Sir Walter went up to Nolan with marked courtesy, saying: 'Shall we go outside now and get this business done?'

Dawn had lifted, leaving a wide chasm of white between a great grey cloud and the great grey moorland, beyond which the tower was outlined against the daybreak and the sea. Something in its plain and primitive shape vaguely suggested the dawn in the first days of the earth; in some prehistoric time when even the colours were hardly created; when there was only blank daylight between cloud and clay. These dead hues were only relieved by one spot of gold: the spark of the candle alight in the window of the lonely tower, and burning on into broadening daylight. As the group of detectives, followed by a cordon of policemen, spread out into a crescent to cut off all escape, the light in the tower flashed as if it were moved for a moment, and then went out. They guessed the man inside had realized the daylight and blown out his candle.

'There are other windows, aren't there?' said Morton. 'And a door, of course, somewhere round the corner – only a round tower has no corners.'

'Another example of my small suggestion,' observed Wilson quietly. 'That queer tower was the first thing I saw when I came to these parts, and I can tell you a little more about it, or, at any rate, the outside of it. There are four windows altogether; one a little way from this one, but just out of sight. Those are both on the ground floor, and so is the third on the other side, making a sort of triangle. But the fourth is just above the third, and I suppose it looks on an upper floor.'

'It's only a sort of loft, reached by a ladder,' said Nolan. 'I've played in the place when I was a child. It's no more than an empty shell.' And his face grew sadder, thinking, perhaps, of the tragedy of his country and the part that he played in it.

'The man must have got a sort of table and chair, at any rate,' said Wilson; 'but no doubt he could have got those from some cottage. If I might make a suggestion, sir, I think we ought to approach all the five entrances at once, so to speak. One of us should go to the door and one to each window; Macbride here has a ladder for the upper window.'

Mr. Horne Fisher, the languid secretary, turned to his distinguished relative and spoke for the first time.

'I am rather a convert to the Cockney school of psychology,' he said, in an almost inaudible voice.

The others seemed to feel the same influence in different ways, for the group began to break up in the manner indicated. Morton moved towards the window immediately in front of them, where the hidden outlaw had apparently just snuffed the candle; Nolan, a little farther westward, to the next window; while Wilson, followed by Macbride with the ladder, went round to the two windows at the back. Sir Walter Carey himself, followed by his secretary, began to walk round towards the only door, to demand admittance in a more regular fashion.

'He will be armed, of course?' remarked Sir Walter casually.

'By all accounts,' repled Horne Fisher, 'he can do more with a candlestick than most men with a pistol. But he is pretty sure to have the pistol, too.'

Even as he spoke the question was answered with a tongue of thunder. Morton had just placed himself in front of the nearest window, his broad shoulders blocking the aperture. For an instant it was lit from within as with red fire, followed by a thundering throng of echoes. The square shoulders seemed to alter in shape, and the sturdy figure collapsed among the tall, rank grasses at the foot of the tower. A puff of smoke floated from the window like a little cloud. The two men behind rushed to the spot and raised him; but he was dead.

Sir Walter straightened himself and called out something that was lost in another noise of firing; it was possible that the police were already avenging their comrade from the other side. Fisher had already raced round to the next window, and a new cry of astonishment from him brought his patron to the same spot.

Nolan, the Irish policeman, had also fallen, sprawling all his great length in the grass, and it was red with blood. He was still alive when they reached him, but there was death on his face, and he was only able to make a final gesture telling them that all was over, and with a broken word and a heroic effort motioning them on to where his other comrades were besieging the back of the tower. Stunned by these rapid and repeated shocks, the two men could only vaguely obey the gesture, and finding their way to the other windows at the back, they found a scene equally startling, if less final and tragic. The other two officers were not dead or mortally wounded, but Macbride lay with a broken leg and his ladder on top of him, evidently thrown down from the top window of the tower; while Wilson lay on his face, quite still, as if stunned, with his red head among the grey and silver of the sea-holly. In him, however, the impotence was but momentary, for he began to move and rise as the others came round the tower.

'My God, it's like an explosion,' cried Sir Walter; and, indeed, it was the only word for this unearthly energy by which one man had been able to deal death or destruction on three sides of the same small triangle at the same instant.

Wilson had already scrambled to his feet and with splendid energy flew again at the window, revolver in hand. He fired twice into the opening, and then disappeared in his own smoke; but the thud of his feet and the shock of a falling chair told them that the intrepid Londoner had managed at last to leap into the room. Then followed a curious silence, and Sir Walter, walking to the window through the thinning smoke, looked into the hollow shell of the ancient tower. Except for Wilson, staring around him, there was nobody there.

The inside of the tower was a single empty room, with nothing but a plain wooden chair and a table on which were pens, ink, and paper, and the candlestick. Half way up the high wall there was a rude timber platform under the upper window: a small loft which was more like a large shelf. It was reached only by a ladder, and it seemed to be as bare as the bare walls. Wilson completed his survey of the place, and then went and stared at the things on the table. Then he silently pointed with his lean forefinger at the open page of the large notebook. The writer had suddenly stopped writing, even in the middle of a word.

'I said it was like an explosion.' said Sir Walter Carey at last. 'And really the man himself seems to have suddenly exploded. But he has blown himself up somehow, without touching the tower. He's burst more like a bubble than a bomb.'

'He has touched more valuable things than the tower,' said Wilson gloomily.

There was a long silence, and then Sir Walter said seriously: 'Well, Mr. Wilson, I am not a detective. And these unhappy happenings have left you in charge of that branch of the business. We all lament the cause of this; but I should like to say that I myself have the strongest confidence in your capacity for carrying on the work. What do you think we should do next?'

Wilson seemed to rouse himself from his depression, and acknowledged the speaker's words with a warmer civility than he had hitherto shown to anybody. He called in a few of the police to assist in routing out the interior, leaving the rest to spread themselves in a search-party outside.

'I think,' he said, 'the first thing is to make quite sure about the inside of this place, as it was hardly physically possible for him to have got outside. I suppose poor Nolan would have brought in his banshee, and said it was supernaturally possible. But I've got no use for disembodied spirits when I'm dealing with facts. And the facts before me are an empty tower with a ladder, a chair, and a table.'

'The spiritualists,' said Sir Walter, with a smile, 'would say that spirits could find a great deal of use for a table.'

'I dare say they could if the spirits were on the table, in a bottle,' replied Wilson, with a curl of his pale lip. 'The people round here, when they're all sodden with Irish whisky, may believe in such things. I think they want a little education in this country.'

Horne Fisher's heavy eyelids fluttered in a faint attempt to rise, as if he were tempted to a lazy protest against the contemptuous tone of the investigator.

'The Irish believe far too much in spirits to believe in spiritualism,' he murmured. 'They know too much about 'em. If you want a simple and childlike faith in any spirit that comes along, you can get it in your favourite London.'

'I don't want to get it anywhere,' said Wilson shortly. 'I say I'm dealing with much simpler things than your simple faith; with a table and a chair and a ladder. Now what I want to say about them at the start is this. They are all three made roughly enough of plain wood. But the table and the chair are fairly new and comparatively clean. The ladder is covered with dust, and there is a cobweb under the top rung of it. That means that he borrowed the first two quite recently from some cottage, as we supposed; but the ladder has been a long time in this rotten old dustbin. Probably it was part of the original furniture; an heirloom in this magnificent palace of the Irish kings.'

Again Fisher looked at him under his eyelids, but seemed too sleepy to speak; and Wilson went on with his argument.

'Now it's quite clear that something very odd has just happened in this place. The chances are ten to one, it seems to me, that it had something specially to do with this place. Probably he came here because he could only do it here; it doesn't seem very inviting otherwise. But the man knew it of old; they say it belonged to his family; so that altogether, I think, everything points to something in the construction of the tower itself.'

'Your reasoning seems to me excellent,' said Sir Walter, who was listening attentively. 'But what could it be?'

'You see now what I mean about the ladder,' went on the detective. 'It's the only old piece of furniture here, and the first thing that caught that Cockney eye of mine. But there is something else. That loft up there is a sort of lumber-room without any lumber. So far as I can see, it's as empty as everything else, and as things are, I don't see the use of the ladder leading to it. It seems to me, as I can't find anything unusual down here, that it may pay us to look up there.'

He got briskly off the table on which he was sitting (for the only chair was allotted to Sir Walter) and ran rapidly up the ladder to the platform above. He was soon followed by the others, Mr. Fisher going last, however, with an appearance of considerable nonchalance.

At this stage, however, they were destined to disappointment; Wilson nosed in every corner like a terrier, and examined the roof almost in the posture of a fly; but half an hour afterwards they had to confess that they were still without a clue. Sir Walter's private secretary seemed more and more threatened with inappropriate slumber; and having been the last to climb the ladder, seemed now to lack the energy even to climb down again.

'Come along, Fisher,' called out Sir Walter from below, when the others had regained the floor. 'We must consider whether we'll pull the whole place to pieces to see what it's made of.'

'I'm coming in a minute,' said the voice from the ledge above their heads; a voice somewhat suggestive of an inarticulate yawn.

'What are you waiting for?' asked Sir Walter impatiently. 'Can you see anything there?'

'Well, yes, in a way,' replied the voice vaguely. 'In fact I see it quite plain now.'

'What is it?' asked Wilson sharply, from the table on which he sat kicking his heels restlessly.

'Well it's a man,' said Horne Fisher.

Wilson bounded off the table as if he had been kicked off it.

'What do you mean?' he cried. 'How can you possibly see a man?'

'I can see him through the window,' replied the secretary mildly. 'I see him coming across the moor. He's making a bee-line across the open country towards this tower. He evidently means to pay us a visit. And considering who it seems to be, perhaps it would be more polite if we were all at the door to receive him.' And the secretary came in a leisurely manner down the ladder.

'Who it seems to be!' repeated Wilson in astonishment.

'Well, I think it's the man you call Prince Michael,' observed Mr. Fisher airily. 'In fact, I'm sure it is. I've seen the police portraits of him.'

There was a dead silence, and Sir Walter's usually steady brain seemed to go round like a windmill.

'But hang it all,' he said at last, 'even supposing his own explosion could have thrown him half a mile away, without passing through any of the windows, and left him alive enough for a country walk – even then, why the devil should he walk in this direction? The murderer does not generally revisit the scene of his crime so rapidly as all that.'

'He doesn't know yet that it is the scene of his crime,' answered Horne Fisher.

'What on earth do you mean? You credit him with rather singular absence of mind.'

'Well, the truth is, it isn't the scene of his crime,' said Fisher, and went and looked out of the window.

There was another silence, and then Sir Walter said quietly: 'What sort of notion have you really got in your head Fisher? Have you developed a new theory about how this fellow escaped out of the ring round him?'

'He never escaped at all,' answered the man at the window, without turning round. 'He never escaped out of the ring because he was never inside the ring. He was not in this tower at all; at least, not when we were surrounding it.'

He turned and leaned his back against the window; but in spite of his usual listless manner, they almost fancied that the face in the shadow was a little pale.

'I began to guess something of the sort when we were some way from the tower,' he said. 'Did you notice that sort of flash or flicker the candle gave before it was extinguished? I was almost certain it was only the last leap the flame gives when a candle burns itself out. And then I came into this room, and I saw that.'

He pointed at the table, and Sir Walter caught his breath with a sort of curse at his own blindness. For the candle in the candlestick had obviously burnt itself away to nothing, and left him, mentally at least, very completely in the dark.

'Then there is a sort of mathematical question,' went on Fisher, leaning back in his limp way and looking up at the bare walls, as if tracing imaginary diagrams there. 'It's not so easy for a man in the middle of a triangle to face all three sides; but it's easier for a man in the third angle to face the other two at the same moment, especially if they are at the base of an isosceles. I am sorry if it sounds like a lecture on geometry, but – '

'I'm afraid we have no time for it,' said Wilson coldly. 'If this man is really coming back, I must give my orders at once.'

'I think I'll go on with it, though,' observed Fisher, staring at the roof with an insolent serenity.

'I must ask you, Mr. Fisher, to let me conduct my inquiry on my own lines,' said Wilson firmly. 'I am the officer in charge now.'

'Yes,' remarked Horne Fisher softly, but with an accent that somehow chilled the hearer, 'yes. But why?'

Sir Walter was staring, for he had never seen his rather lackadaisical young friend look like that before. Fisher was looking at Wilson with lifted lids, and the eyes under them seemed to have shed or shifted a film, as do the eyes of an eagle.

'Why are you the officer in charge now?' he asked. 'Why can you conduct the inquiry on your own lines now? How did it come about, I wonder, that the elder officers are not here to interfere with anything you do?'

Nobody spoke, and nobody can say how soon anyone would have collected his wits to speak, when a noise came from without. It was the heavy and hollow sound of a blow upon the door of the tower, and to their shaken spirits it sounded strangely like the hammer of doom.

The wooden door of the tower moved on its rusty hinges under the hand that struck it, and Prince Michael came into the room. Nobody had the smallest doubt about his identity. His light clothes, though frayed with his adventures, were the fine and almost foppish cut, and he wore a pointed beard or imperial, perhaps as a further reminiscence of Louis Napoleon; but he was a much taller and more graceful man than his prototype. Before anyone could speak, he had silenced everyone for an instant with a slight but splendid gesture of hospitality.

'Gentlemen,' he said, 'this is a poor place now, but you are heartily welcome.'

Wilson was the first to recover, and he took a stride towards the new-comer.

'Michael O'Neill, I arrest you in the King's name for the murder of Francis Morton and James Nolan. It is my duty to warn you – '

'No, no, Mr. Wilson,' cried Fisher, suddenly, 'you shall not commit a third murder.'

Sir Walter Carey rose from his chair, which fell over with a crash behind him.

'What does all this mean?; he called out in an authoritative manner.

'It means,' said Fisher, 'that this man, Hooker Wilson, as soon as he put his head in at that window, killed his two comrades who had put their heads in at the other windows, by means of firing across the empty room. That is what it means. And if you want to know, count how many times he is supposed to have fired, and then count the charges left in his revolver.'

Wilson, who was still sitting on the table, abruptly put a hand out for the weapon that lay beside him. But the next movement was the most unexpected of all, for the Prince, standing in the doorway, passed suddenly from the dignity of a statue to the swiftness of an acrobat, and rent the revolver out of the detective's hand.

'You dog,' he cried. 'So you are the type of English truth, as I am of Irish tragedy; you who have come to kill me, wading through the blood of your brethren. If they had fallen in a feud on the hillside, it would be called murder, and yet your sin might be forgiven you. But I, who am innocent, I was to be slain with ceremony. There would be long speeches and patient judges listening to my vain plea of innocence, noting down my despair and disregarding it. Yes, that is what I call assassination, But killing may be no murder; there is one shot left in this little gun, and I know where it should go.'

Wilson turned quickly on the table, and even as he turned he twisted in agony; for Michael shot him through the body where he sat, so that he tumbled off the table like lumber.

The police rushed to lift him; Sir Walter stood speechless; and then with a strange and weary gesture, Horne Fisher spoke.

'You are indeed a type of the Irish tragedy,' he said. 'You are entirely in the right, and you have put yourself in the wrong.'

The Prince's face was like marble for a space; then there dawned in his eyes a light not unlike that of despair. He laughed suddenly and flung the smoking pistol on the ground.

'I am indeed in the wrong,' he said. 'I have committed a crime that may justly bring a curse on me and my children.'

Horne Fisher did not seem entirely satisfied with this very sudden repentance; he kept his eyes on the man and only said in a low voice; 'What crime do you mean?'

'I have helped English justice,' replied Prince Michael. 'I have avenged your King's officers; I have done the work of his hangman. For that, truly, I deserve to be hanged.'

And he turned to the police with a gesture that did not so much surrender to them, but rather command them to arrest him.

This was the story that Horne Fisher told to Harold March, the journalist, many years after, in a little but luxurious restaurant near Piccadilly. He had invited March to dinner some time after the affair he called 'The Face in the Target,' and the conversation had naturally turned on that mystery and afterwards on earlier memories of Fisher's life; and the way in which he had been led to study problems as those of Prince Michael. Horne Fisher was fifteen years older; his thin hair had faded to frontal baldness, and his long thin hands dropped less with affectation and more with fatigue. And he told the story of the Irish adventure of his youth because it recorded the first occasion on which he had ever come in contact with crime, or discovered how darkly and how terribly crime can be entangled with law.

'Hooker Wilson was the first criminal I ever knew, and he was a policeman,' explained Fisher, twirling his wine-glass. 'And all my life has been a mixed-up business of the sort. He was a man of very real talent, and perhaps genius, and well worth studying both as a detective and a criminal. His white face and red hair were typical of him, for he was one of those who are cold and yet on fire for fame; and he could control his anger but not ambition. He swallowed the snubs of his superiors in that first quarrel, though he boiled with resentment; but when he suddenly saw the two heads dark against the dawn and framed in the two windows, he could not miss the chance, not only of revenge, but of the removal of the two obstacles to his promotion. He was a dead shot, and counted on silencing both, though proof against him would have been hard in any case. But, as a matter of fact, he had a narrow escape in the case of Nolan, who lived just long enough to say 'Wilson' and point. We thought he was summoning help for his comrade, but he was really denouncing his murderer. After that it was easy to throw down the ladder above him (for a man up a ladder cannot see clearly what is below and behind) and to throw himself on the ground as another victim of the catastrophe.

'But there was mixed up with his murderous ambition a real belief, not only in his own talents, but in his own theories. He did believe in what he called a fresh eye, and he did want scope for fresh methods. There was something in his view; but it failed where such things commonly fail, because the fresh eye cannot see the unseen. It is true about the ladder and the scarecrow, but not about the life and the soul; and he made a bad mistake about what a man like Michael would do when he heard a woman scream. All Michael's very vanity and vain-glory made him rush out at once; he would have walked into Dublin Castle for a lady's glove. Call it his pose or what you will, but he would have done it. What happened when he met her is another story, and one we may never know; but from tales I've heard since, they must have been reconciled. Wilson was wrong there, but there was something, for all that, in his notion that the new-comer sees most, and that the man on the spot may know too much to know anything. He was right about some things. He was right about me.'

'About you?' asked March.

'I am the man who knows too much to know anything, or, at any rate, to do anything,' said Horne Fisher. 'I don't mean especially about Ireland. I mean about England. I mean about the whole way we are governed, and perhaps the only way we can be governed. You asked me just now what became of the survivors of that tragedy. Well, Wilson recovered, and we managed to persuade him to retire. But we had to pension that damnable murderer more magnificently than any hero who ever fought for England. I managed to save Michael from the worst, but we had to send that perfectly innocent man to penal servitude for a crime we know he never committed; but it was only afterwards that we could connive in a sneakish way at his escape. And Sir Walter Carey is Prime Minister of this country, which he would probably never have been if the truth had been told of such a horrible scandal in his department. It might have done for us altogether in Ireland; it would certainly have done for him. And he is my father's old friend, and has always smothered me with kindness. I am too tangled up with the whole thing, you see, and I was certainly never born to set it right. You look distressed, not to say shocked, and I'm not at all offended at it. Let us change the subject by all means, if you like. What do you think of this Burgundy? It's rather a discovery of mine, like the restaurant itself.'

As he proceeded to talk earnestly and luxuriantly on all the wines of the world; on which subject, also, some moralist would consider that he knew too much.

SOURCES AND NOTES

'A Defence of Detective Stories' first published as 'The Value of Detective Stories' in *The Speaker,* June 22, 1901; collected in *The Defendant* (London: R. Brimley Johnson, 1901). Written some years before Chesterton himself attempted a detective story.

'The Man Who Shot the Fox' published in *Ellery Queen's Mystery Magazine,* Vol. 8, No. 32 (July, 1946); original magazine publication not given.

'The Five Swords' (first magazine publication unknown) was selected by Chesterton as his favourite of his own stories for *My Best Story* (London: Faber, 1929). 'The Vanishing Prince' and 'The Tower of Treason' first published in *The Storyteller* in February, 1920 and February, 1924 respectively. These three stories collected in *The Man Who Knew Too Much, and other stories* (London: Cassell, 1922), but the first two were omitted from the US edition.

'The Noticeable Conduct of Professor Chadd' first published in *The Idler,* 1904; collected in *The Club of Queer Trades* (London and New York: Harper Brothers, 1905), illustrated by the author.

'The Moderate Murderer' first published in *Cassell's Magazine,* April, 1929; collected in *Four Faultless Felons* (London: Cassell, 1930).

'The Purple Jewel' first published in *The Storyteller,* March, 1929; collected in *The Poet and the Lunatics: episodes in the life of Gabriel Gale* (London: Cassell, 1929).